taylor five

Ann Halam is the penname of Gwyneth Jones,
who also writes science fiction and fantasy for
adults. She was born and raised in Manchester,
and after graduating from Sussex University
spent some years travelling throughout South
East Asia. She now lives in Brighton with her
husband and son, but spends   she
can heading o

Other books by the same author

The Haunting of Jessica Raven
The Fear Man
The Powerhouse
Crying in the Dark
The N.I.M.R.O.D. Conspiracy
Don't Open Your Eyes
Dr Franklin's Island

taylor five

Ann Halam

First published in Great Britain in 2002
as a Dolphin paperback
by Orion Children's Books
a division of the Orion Publishing Group Ltd
Orion House
5 Upper St Martin's Lane
London WC2H 9EA

Reprinted 2003

A catalogue record for this book is available
from the British Library

Typeset at The Spartan Press Ltd,
Lymington, Hants

Printed in Great Britain by
Clays Ltd, St Ives plc

ISBN 1 85881 792 7

for Catherine Sinclair-Jones

One

Mum and Dad couldn't come to the airport to meet Donny, but that was okay: he would understand. Lucia Fernandez and Udin the driver came with Tay instead. They were in luck on Airport Road and got through the police check-points with no delay, which meant they had ages to wait before the plane from Singapore arrived. Lucia found someone to talk to at the immigration desk. Udin got himself a cup of coffee and a newspaper. Tay walked around, looking at the familiar souvenir shops, sniffing the spicy-food scents from the cafeteria bar – a thin girl with golden-brown hair, wearing a blue cotton dress, a Yankees baseball cap and desert boots. She felt slightly nervous. This was the first time she'd been in a public place since the story broke. No one was supposed to know who she was – but she almost expected a horde of journalists to leap out, waving cameras and microphones. Thankfully, no one paid any attention. Here in the sleepy quiet of a tiny tropical airport, no one knew or cared that Taylor Walker was one of the five teenagers whose existence had just been announced, who were the most astonishing people on the planet.

Donny and Tay had lived in Kandah State, a small independent country on the north coast of the giant island

1

of Borneo, since Donny was five and Tay was seven. Their parents were the wardens of an Orang-Utan Refuge, out in the wilds of one of the last great rainforests. Ben and Mary Walker both worked for an international company called Lifeforce, which financed the Refuge. To some people it would have seemed a hard and lonely life for the two English children, but they loved it. The forest was such a fantastic place to live. It had been a cruel blow when their parents had decided that Donny had to go to school in Singapore. But it was fine now. They just looked forward through each term to having a brilliant time together in the holidays.

Would things be different, this summer?

Tay visited the cheap stalls, with the stacks of ugly imitation Dyak carvings that never seemed to get sold; and the Instant Tailoring shop, where the Chinese tailor-women whizzed the cloth through their sewing machines at incredible speed. They would sew you a perfect made-to-measure shirt in about ten minutes. She had a Coke at the ice-cream parlour, where rich Muslim girls from the airport suburbs (a very classy area of Kota Kandah, capital city of Kandah State) sat gossiping, some of them in head-to-toe white embroidered veils. Donny won't be different, she was telling herself. He won't care. But she had butterflies in her stomach.

There was a sarong that she would *really* have liked to buy, in Mrs Su's Genuine Dyak Crafts Centre. It was heavy and hand-woven, with swirls and thorny curves in gold thread, on shades of dark red silk. She could imagine her mum wearing this. Tay's mum hardly ever got a chance to wear anything but jungle kit, but she loved beautiful clothes. Mrs Su, the Chinese lady who owned the shop, came over as Tay stroked the shimmering folds, with a smile that showed

2

all the gold in her teeth. She took the sarong and deftly unfolded it.

'Ve'y nice? Eh?'

'It's *lovely*,' sighed Tay.

'You old customer, young lady, I make you a special price. Not New York price, not airport price. Nah, real price.'

Tay knew that even the 'real price' of the best hand-woven gold-thread work was way beyond her means. 'I can't afford it, Mrs Su. I've only got six hundred dollars left in my bank account, and I owe most of it to my dad.'

Six hundred Kandah dollars meant about fifty English pounds. 'Ha,' said Mrs Su, and shook her head. 'Okay, you tell your daddy, huh? Mrs Su got the best silk-work, special price. You here to meet your brother, home from school, eh?'

Tay grinned. 'Yes.' Most of the foreigners who lived in Kandah were 'oilies' – oil rig people – or 'chippies' – which meant they worked for the logging companies – and none stayed for long. The Walkers had been at the Refuge for seven years. Mrs Su knew Donny and Tay well. Whenever they came to the airport they came into her shop, to talk to her, and she gave them strange, hard Chinese candies.

The old lady folded up the sarong. 'Why *you* never go to school, Tay, you so grown up now? Don't want an education?'

'I'm getting an education,' said Tay. 'I work at home, that's all.'

'Huh. A smart girl like you; ought to be in school. Got to learn to compete, make your way, be tough. Some things you can't learn from books.'

Two teenage girls came in. One of them, about Tay's age, was wearing a sarong and blouse – the traditional Kandah

3

dress, but very smart – and a Muslim headscarf. The other, who looked about sixteen, was bare-headed. She had her glossy black hair cut short and feathered, and she was dressed in the 'Wild West' style that was the height of fashion in Kandah City – boot-cut faded jeans, a beaded belt, and a Western-style shirt with fringes and silver buttons. Tay instantly loved the shirt.

The girls whispered to each other, and giggled.

Tay didn't have the kind of life that would let her get to know girls her own age: and she didn't mind. She loved living in the magical wilderness of the deep forest. But suddenly she felt a terrible pang, watching those two strangers and thinking she would never, *never*, have a life like theirs. She would never be able to meet her friends and go out with them, just to have an ice-cream and hang around the shops, gossiping, trying things on . . . She would always have the horrible weight of her secret identity hanging round her neck, always afraid someone would find out—

Tay and Mrs Su had been speaking in English. The girls were speaking Malay – but Tay knew the Kandanese dialect of that language very well. As they came near, she could understand every word. There was a sexy pop star poster on one of the cheap stalls that the younger girl wanted to buy, only she knew their dad wouldn't let her put it up in her bedroom. And someone at school had done something really *bodoh* (stupid) . . .

'What wrong?' said the old lady, peering at Tay. Mrs Su didn't miss much. 'You don't take offence at old Mrs Su? You got a pain?'

'No, Mrs Su,' said Tay. 'I'm just worried about something.'

Mrs Su sighed, and nodded as she put the sarong back on the display shelf.

'Ah, understand. Your mother and father worried, everyone worried, even children now. Hard times for me too. No one buying. Hard times for everyone.'

Tay went out of the shop, but not before Mrs Su had insisted she take a handful of brightly wrapped sweets from the jar by the cash register. The afternoon plane from Singapore had arrived, and the passengers were streaming into the arrivals hall. For a moment, Tay felt a weird jolt of fear. Something had gone wrong, because she couldn't see Donny . . . But no, she was being stupid. There he was, talking to some people he must have met on the plane. He saw her, and his whole face lit up.

'Hey! There's my sister!'

He came bouncing out of the crowd and leapt up to her, grinning from ear to ear, a twelve-year-old boy with blue eyes and black hair, and the personality of a crazy puppy. They hugged, and backed off so they could look at each other.

'I'm taller than you!' he crowed, 'I *knew* I'd be taller than you, these holidays.'

'Nearly,' said Tay, measuring, and finding her nose still about half a centimetre higher. 'Nearly as tall, and twice as daft.' They gripped hands, did the special Tay and Donny twist of their locked fists, broke the grip and knocked knuckles. It was a ritual they had invented years ago, that always had to be used at important moments.

'How's Harimau?' asked Donny, as they made for the one and only baggage carousel.

Harimau was an orang-utan in the graduation class – a young ape who'd reached the stage where he was partly fending for himself. He'd been ill. The reason why Mum wasn't at the airport was because she'd had to go to Half-Way Camp, where the graduation apes had a feeding station, to check on him and see if he needed to be captured and brought in for treatment. Dad wasn't here, because with Mum out in the forest he couldn't leave the Refuge HQ. One of the wardens had to be on site at all times, especially the way things were at the moment.

'Mum thinks it isn't serious. Oh, and Genevieve's been promoted to graduation class. We're going to Half-Way to release her, next week. We'll camp there for a couple of nights, so you'll probably see Harimau—'

Lucia came to join them. They waited for Donny's bags, Donny and Tay exchanging a babble of news, as if they hadn't spoken to each other in years. They jabbered like monkeys, Lucia complained. Scatterbrains! If she'd hadn't been there they would have let Donny's things go rolling away to the Lost Airport Luggage Dimension, never to be heard of again . . . Not that it would have made much difference. No matter how people hassled him, he never packed properly. He always ended up back here with a fistful of odd socks and nothing else.

They collected the bags, including the Refuge mail drop (which had come on the scheduled flight, because their helicopter delivery had been cancelled). Then they un-earthed Udin from a haze of cigarette smoke, and set off happily for home.

Everything went fine until they reached the outskirts of Kandah city centre, where they wanted to turn right, and head into the interior. There they found that the forest road had been closed while they were at the airport. Another terrorist incident. The police were at the junction, telling people they had to go through the city centre and be searched. With many groans and grumbles people com-plied, but of course this meant that the city centre was gridlocked. The Land Rover crawled, and finally the queue stopped moving entirely. Udin went to investigate. He believed that the prestige of the Lifeforce orang-utan Refuge would get them special treatment, if he talked to the right policeman. Minutes passed. Lucia went to see what had happened to Udin. More minutes passed.

At last Lucia and Udin came back, hot and gloomy.

'They would let us through, but they can't,' said Udin. 'Everything is completely, completely stuck.'

'It'll be an hour, they say,' said Lucia. 'Minimum. Probably two.'

'But *why*?' demanded Tay. 'What's happened? Why was the road closed?'

The others shrugged. 'It's the rebels,' said Udin, as if that answered everything.

'It's not worth worrying about,' said Lucia. 'We just have to be patient.'

Tay groaned. 'Do we have to stay in the Land Rover? I've got my phone.'

'No,' said Lucia. 'Give it an hour, then call me and see how things are going. Or I'll call you, if we get through this, and you can meet us in the ferryboat car park.'

The children walked down to the river, past the eye-watering stink of the midden by the fruit and vegetable market, and across the elegant old footbridge into the modern part of the city. 'Is it going to be like this the whole time?' asked Donny, looking worried. Like a puppy, he was easily smacked down: but thankfully he bounced back just as easily. 'No one told me Kandah had gone all horrible. Why didn't anyone say?'

'I suppose we're used to it. You get used to it. Anyway, it hasn't been *bad*. This hold-up is the worst thing that's happened. Everything's fine at home.'

They both knew what the problem was . . . more or less.

7

Most of Borneo was part of either Malaysia or Indonesia: Kandah State was squashed between these two great nations. The Sultan of Kandah wanted to stay independent; the rebels wanted to change things. Some of them wanted Kandah to join Indonesia, some wanted to join Malaysia. Some of them were Communists, and wanted Kandah to be Communist. They fought with each other, and they fought with the government. Terrifying forest fires were started. Remote little towns and villages were ransacked, like frontier towns in the Wild West being overrun by outlaws. The situation had been going on for years. Usually it all happened in the wild, deep interior, and the people of Kandah City Region only heard about it on the news. Occasionally the action would move nearer, and then there would be delays, searches, roads closed and police check-points.

Tay could remember one time, soon after the Walkers had come to Kandah, when Donny was only five, when they'd been stranded at the Refuge for weeks, living on tinned food, with no deliveries, and soldiers in trucks driving around on the forest tracks. But even then, nothing terrible had happened.

'Things will calm down again. They always do. Mum and Dad aren't worried.'

'Oh no!' exclaimed Donny, stopping in shock, halfway over the bridge. 'I forgot to go and see Mrs Su! And there's police everywhere, so we can't go back!'

'Calm down. I just *told* you, it's nothing serious. You can see her next time anyone has to meet a plane. Anyway, I went to see her for you. Look, I got some candy.'

They walked on, doggedly sucking bitter-as-vinegar candied plums. Neither of them liked the taste, but Mrs Su's candy was a tradition. It was part of Donny's homecoming.

Now the modern glass and concrete towers of the city centre sprang up on either side, and the afternoon felt even hotter. They passed the Mercedes car showroom, where they stopped to drool over the beautiful, fantastically expensive cars; and the department stores where fashionable modern clothes filled the plate glass windows in tempting array. Tay told Donny about the gold-thread sarong at Mrs Su's. It was Mum's birthday very soon, and Donny confessed he hadn't bought her a present. He'd brought home something that he'd made in art class, which he hoped she'd like instead: a calendar and letter holder made out of bamboo and papier-mâché, but he was afraid it might have suffered, travelling in his luggage.

'It's in the shape of a tree-frog. I think it's quite good . . . I hope it's not broken.'

Knowing Donny's method of packing, Tay feared the worst.

'Haven't you any cash left at all? You had plenty of pocket-money.'

'It just sort of went,' said Donny sadly. 'I don't know how, but it's all gone.'

'Okay, look. You can come in with me. I've mail-ordered something really good. You can share it with me, and pay me back.'

'How much?'

'It's costing me four fifty, which is most of my bank account until next month. Say you put in one hundred? I'll show you what it is, in the catalogue on the net, when we get home. It's an excellent present, trust me.'

Donny grinned, delighted to have a reason to cheer up.

'Done! And I honestly will pay you back.'

'You bet you will, bro'.'

There was no sign of the Land Rover in the ferry car park.

Tay called Lucia, and was told the queue was moving, but *pelan, pelan*, which meant *slowly*, but also meant *so relax* – a favourite local expression. The Kandanese never got stressed over things (unless you counted the rebels, who seemed to stress enough for everyone).

'They'd better hurry up,' said Donny, grinning, 'or we'll be driving in the dark.'

'*Pelan, pelan*,' said Tay. 'You're not in Singapore any more, kid. This is Kandah, remember? The pace is slow, even in terrorist emergencies.'

Really, the children loved driving in the dark. It was the adults who could never see the romance of forging through the forest by night.

'Maybe we'll meet a giant monitor lizard,' suggested Donny hopefully. 'Like the one that attacked Dad that night, in the old Land Rover, when we got a flat tyre?'

'He was changing the wheel,' agreed Tay. It was a family legend. 'At midnight, and a huge monitor lizard burst out of the bushes and *ran over him*.'

'It was as big as a tank!' said Donny, laughing. 'It nearly broke his ribs!'

'It was three metres long, at least. Probably *five*—' (The lizard had grown bigger, every time Dad told the tale).

They went over to the river wharf, bought a green coconut from the coconut man's stall and sat dangling their legs and passing it between them, sipping the cool, refreshing coconut milk through a straw. Yellow butterflies fluttered among the drifts of blue water hyacinth; someone was mending a boat, pop music on the radio. Everything in the familiar scene was as it should be: the hot, bright modern towers and the little peasant food-stalls clustering at their feet, the big brown swirling river with its old warehouses and new hotels; the rafts and motor boats plying to and fro . . . But although Donny hadn't even mentioned the secret, Tay felt strange. She felt like a painted cardboard figure, like a package made to look like a girl, with something hardly human inside it. Like someone who didn't belong in this quiet world; or any other place.

About five o'clock, the Land Rover turned up. Tay and Donny climbed in and they drove away, through the straggle of shanty town around the tropic city and into the thrilling dusk of the forest, just as the fruitbats came out for their evening prowl, flapping up out of the sunset like an army of vampires.

The place that Tay and Donny called home was a broad forest clearing, surrounded by the orang-utan reserve where no human settlement was allowed. Donny and Tay and their mum and dad lived in the main buildings, which were set around an open square. Their house was built like a Dyak longhouse, raised on wooden pillars above the ground, with a high-ridged roof and a shady verandah running along the front. The labs, the Refuge offices and the telecoms suite were on the square too. The other staff had cottages of their own, scattered among flowerbeds, stands of bamboo and blossoming shade trees. In the open space in the middle of the square there were canopied swinging chairs, a table and benches, a skittle run, and a telescope. People gathered there in the cool evenings to eat together, to play games or talk, or to watch a movie (projected on to a whitewashed wall of the office block).

There were twelve or fifteen baby apes and 'children' at any time, besides the 'graduates' who were nearly independent but still coming to the feeding stations. Each of the young orphans had an individual human carer. There was also a research team, a veterinary team, technicians and support staff; and there were usually a couple of visiting scientists, who came from all over the world to work here at the Lifeforce Refuge and observe the great red apes. (Most of the carers were also students. Lucia was one of these: she was a zoology graduate from the Philippines.) It was a close-knit little international village, of about thirty or forty people, in which Donny and Tay were the only human children.

When the Land Rover reached home, around ten o'clock at night, Dad was at the gates in the perimeter fence to greet them. Mum was back from Half-Way Camp, and the central square was ablaze with lights. Everyone seemed to be there, from Minah the cook to the very shy visiting German zoologist who hardly spoke (he got on better with animals than with humans). Donny put on his sunglasses, struck a celebrity pose and said 'Please, please, no autographs.' The grown-ups laughed and said they weren't interested in *him*, they were here for the mail drop! When you live in the wilds, no matter how good your communication system is, books, letters and newspapers are like gold-dust. The big parcel of newspapers, journals and disks was pulled out of its bag, with cheers and whoops, and tumbled on the communal table—

There, on the front of the *Singapore Straits Times*, was the story, in banner headlines:

BIOTECH GIANT LIFEFORCE
ANNOUNCES HUMAN CLONES!
THEY'RE TEENAGERS ALREADY!
THEY ARE LIVING AMONG US!

Tay froze. She tried to stop her face from showing anything, but she couldn't help it.

Donny took off his sunglasses, and said, 'Oh, sorry, Tay. I didn't think.'

'What's the problem?' said Tay. 'I'm famous, that's all. Aren't I lucky.'

She blundered out of the square, hurried along the dark verandah and shut herself in her room.

Mum came along later, and so did someone else, who knocked and went away – probably Donny. But she pretended she was asleep, and wouldn't answer them.

Morning came early to the clearing. Before six o'clock the gibbons in the bamboo stand outside Tay's bedroom window began hooting and singing to greet the new day. She lay listening to them, the way she did every morning; remembering that Donny was home, and wondering why she didn't feel happy. Then it came back to her.

She got up, showered and went along to the Walkers' family kitchen, feeling ashamed of her behaviour last night. Donny was eating breakfast with Mum and Dad. They all looked at her uneasily, and said 'Hello, Tay,' 'Good morning, Tay,' in subdued voices. Tay fetched herself a glass of juice and a sweet roll from the fridge (all perishable food had to be kept in the fridge, to protect it from the ants).

'How is Harimau?' she said, casually. 'I forgot to ask.'

'He's fine,' said Mum. 'Just a touch of diarrhoea. No sign of worms, but he might have an amoebic parasite. I have a sample to analyse—'

'*Mum*,' protested Donny. 'Do you mind? I'm eating!'

'You'd better get used to it,' said Dad. 'City-slicker. Diarrhoea and worms is all we talk about here, except for tropical ulcers—' He grinned at Tay, who didn't grin back.

13

'What are you two going to do today?' Mum asked, hopefully. 'First day of the holidays, I bet you have something planned for him, Tay, don't you?'

'No. I have homework to finish,' said Tay. 'Even famous freaks have homework.'

She rinsed her glass and plate, and walked out.

She went to the schoolroom. Until Donny started at his boarding school they'd both done their lessons here, in this airy, high-ceilinged room with the polished wooden floor and the tall cupboards full of books, art materials, and science equipment. No expense spared, she thought bitterly, looking at all this wealth. It's as if I was dying.

She sat down at her computer, and rested her chin on her hands.

She'd been seven when Mum and Dad told her the truth about herself. Not the whole truth, of course: she wouldn't have been able to understand . . . They'd told her that she was a test-tube baby, and explained what that meant. Though she'd come out of Mummy's tummy, the little egg that had turned into Tay had come from somebody else – and that 'somebody else' was Mummy and Daddy's best friend, Pam Taylor. Pam couldn't have babies of her own, and neither could Mummy (that's what they'd thought, at the time). So they'd decided to have Tay, each of them doing the part of having-a-baby that they could do . . . Tay hadn't been too upset. She liked Pam very much. As long as she was still Mummy and Daddy's little girl, and Donny was still her brother, she didn't mind if Pam was sort of her second mum. But that had been seven years ago, half her lifetime ago—

Tay and Donny Walker were Lifeforce kids. Their parents were wildlife wardens now, but they'd worked for the biotech company as scientists before that. Tay had never

14

been frightened by the idea that she had come out of a test-tube. It had never struck her as odd that she didn't go to school, either. She much preferred working at home and sharing Mum and Dad's adventures. Before Borneo, there'd been a post in Geneva. Before Geneva, there'd been Canada: she'd never known any other way of life. Her classmates in the online international school were dead impressed that she had Pam for a godmother (they didn't know about the test-tube baby part: it was none of their business), because Dr Pam Taylor was head of Lifeforce's conservation projects and a famous scientist: sometimes she was on TV. But, to Tay, having Pam for a grown-up friend – like having Rei van der Hoort, Lifeforce Asia's chief executive, come and stay at the Refuge, and sit up talking with her parents all night – was just normal life.

It wasn't normal that she had to give blood and tissue samples every month, to be sent off to the biotech labs; but it was something Tay'd always had to do. They'd told her it was nothing bad, it was because she was a special sort of test-tube baby, and Lifeforce wanted to monitor her development. It didn't hurt much (although a few times a year the tissue sampling was quite painful); and she had accepted it.

By the time she was twelve she had known exactly what a test-tube baby was, what it meant to say someone was your 'biological' mother and someone else was your 'genetic' mother; and what 'surrogacy' meant . . . Sometimes she'd lain awake at night, wondering about why she *really* had to give the blood and tissue samples, and wishing Mum and Dad would *tell* her, if she had cancer or something. Sometimes she'd brooded about being Pam's 'sort of' baby. A woman's egg cell has to be fertilised by a man's sperm. Who had her father been? Was it her own dad who had provided the sperm? Or someone else, some stranger? And why did Pam decide to have a test-tube baby, and then let the surrogate mother keep the child? Had she decided a child would cramp her famous scientist lifestyle? But Tay, unlike Donny, liked to keep quiet about things that upset or frightened her. She wanted to be a wildlife scientist like her mum and dad, and work somewhere like the Refuge; or maybe do marine conservation biology like Pam. That was her ambition, and that's what was important. When Mum and Dad had tried to talk to her about 'where she had come from', she had always said she thought she knew enough.

Maybe she'd guessed, deep down, that the things they wanted to say would destroy her peace of mind.

Then Mum and Dad had decided that Donny had to go away to school. He hadn't been doing very well. Tay was in top sets for everything in the online international Distance Learning College in which they were both enrolled, but Donny was struggling. He needed a different kind of education. Tay had felt very sorry for him, having to leave the forest and go and live with strangers.

But it was Tay who was the stranger.

A year and a half ago, soon after Donny had left for his first term at the new school, Pam Taylor had come to the Refuge, and Pam and Mum and Dad had told Tay the real truth. She was a *very* special kind of test-tube baby. She had no 'biological' father.

In normal fertility treatment the baby has two parents, and just like any other baby, it will be a new, unique individual, with a combination of the mother's and the father's genes. Tay was different. Lifeforce scientists had taken one of Mary Walker's egg cells, and replaced the nucleus (the package where the cell's DNA is stored) with the nucleus

16

from one of Pam Taylor's ordinary body cells (a bone-marrow cell, in fact). Then they'd treated this egg cell so it would behave as if it had been fertilised. Tay was not just Pam's daughter. She was genetically *the same person* as Pam Taylor.

Lifeforce had created human clones, years before anyone had believed it was possible.

There were four other teenagers like Tay, with four different gene-parents, all of them 'created' at the same time. All of them were Lifeforce kids. Their gene-parents and their surrogate families were part of the Lifeforce company, like everyone else involved with the clone project. The existence of the clones had been kept secret. But now that they were healthy teenagers, and the success of the experiment was beyond doubt, the company thought it was time to break the silence.

Tay's identity would be protected. The company would prove their amazing claim by scientific means: by letting other scientists examine tissue samples from clones and gene-parents. Tay's picture wouldn't be in the papers, and she wouldn't have to appear on TV. She might never even know the names of the other four clones. But Mum and Dad and Pam had thought she ought to know the truth – before the rest of the world found out.

Tay had been stunned and bewildered, but she'd been determined not to get upset. She still felt like the same person she'd always been: but now she didn't have to worry about having cancer. She had an explanation for the blood tests and tissue samples: and maybe she wasn't going to die young . . . Mum and Dad and Pam had been puzzled, but happy, because Tay was so calm. Secretly she'd been very proud that she'd been able to take this bombshell so well. She'd been a Lifeforce kid all her life, she *knew* about the miracles of modern biotech. She'd refused to feel sorry for herself, or weirded out. She'd convinced Mum and Dad, and everyone else that she was fine.

The only thing was that after the big revelation, she'd stopped writing to Pam.

She'd been truly *friends* with her 'test-tube mum'. Wherever Pam's work took her, she had always stayed in e-mail contact. They'd talked on the phone, when they could, as often as if they were friends of the same age. For some reason, that had stopped. Tay hadn't meant it to happen, she just . . . didn't have anything to say.

Since that time, life had carried on as normal. Tay had done her schoolwork, and helped out as much as she was allowed to with the apes. There'd been school holidays, and she'd had great times with Donny. There'd been a visit to England (which Donny and Tay had both hated). There'd been trips to Singapore. Tay had often almost forgotten about the secret, for weeks at a time; and she'd almost started hoping that Lifeforce had decided to keep the clones' existence a secret forever.

But now the news was out, on the TV and on the radio, on the internet and in the newspapers, all over the world. Tay was very thankful that she lived in the middle of the rainforest and she didn't have to know about all the publicity.

She just wished she knew why she suddenly felt so bad.

What does it *mean* to be a clone? How is a clone supposed to feel?

She switched on her computer, chose a picture file and sat looking at video clips of Pam Taylor, shrinking and copying them until the screen was a photomosaic of Pam's tanned face: smiling, laughing, using her hands to talk, the way Pam always did . . . And so did Tay. She clicked with the mouse, enlarging one detail and then another, studying the way Pam's hair grew. The shape of her nose. The colour of her eyes.

Every little bit of me is exactly the same as that. That's *exactly* what I will look like.

Tay knew it was Mum and Dad who'd come into the room before she looked round. It was too late to switch off the screen . . . They sat down, on either side of her.

'Hi,' Mum said, quietly.

'Hi,' said Dad. He took Tay's hand.

'Hi, you,' said Tay. 'I'm all right, honestly. I'm sorry I was snappish.'

'Tay—' said Mum. 'You're not a freak. Everyone you know . . . Everyone in Lifeforce knows you are a wonderful, brave, clever, *excellent* young woman.'

'It's *okay*, Mum. I understand what a big deal it is. I know that me being a clone is an amazing triumph, and it will have huge benefits for medicine, and I'm fine. I just wish . . . Oh, Mum. If I had to be a copy of someone, why couldn't I be a copy of you?'

'It didn't work out that way,' said Mum. 'Tay . . . I was nearly forty, and—'

'We thought we couldn't have children,' said Dad. 'We were contemplating fertility treatment. The clone project came along, and they were asking for volunteers—'

'I wasn't sure, but I tested,' put in Mum. 'I was histo-compatible with one of the donors. You know what that means: I had the right kind of cell profile, like a bio-chemical fingerprint: and the donor turned out to be Pam, who was our dear friend. We thought about it long and hard, but we've been so glad we said yes.'

'Because it gave us *you*,' said Dad. 'Just the way you are. You were a miracle to us.'

19

'And then you had Donny.'

Mum nodded. 'Yes. It sometimes happens. A test-tube pregnancy and then an ordinary one, when there's been unexplained infertility before. No one understands why, not yet. So we had two miracles.'

Every time Mum and Dad told her the story (and they'd told it to her over and over, in different ways, since they'd told her the truth) she could see in their eyes how much they loved her, and how much they wanted her to say that everything was okay.

'In the *Straits Times* it said something about a "human photocopy". I didn't want to read any of it, but I saw that.'

'Well, the *Straits Times* got it wrong,' said Dad. 'You are not a copy. You are an original. It isn't the DNA that counts: it's what you do with it. It's the person. You aren't a "photocopy" of Pam. You are our daughter, and our proudest achievement.'

'Yes,' said Tay. 'And I love you too. True.'

'Do you want to see Pam?' suggested Mum. 'She could be here in a few hours.'

Tay's gene-mother was working on the Marine and Shore Station – another part of the biotech company's conservation work. The floating research lab was moored off the north east coast of Kandah State just now. Tay knew this wasn't an accident. It had been arranged so Pam would be nearby if Tay wanted to see her, when the story broke.

But she didn't want to see Pam.

Not now, maybe not ever . . .

'N-no. I'll talk to her soon, honest. Just not right now. Right now, er, I really do have homework to finish. I ought to have done it before Donny came home—'

'Okay,' said Mum.

'Okay,' said Dad. 'We'll leave you in peace.'

They hugged her, and left her in peace.

The ceiling fans ticked around and around. The Refuge buildings had air-conditioning, but Donny and Tay made it a point of honour not to use it, except in their bedrooms on unbearably sticky nights. It was better to learn to accept the heat as normal, so you could be free and comfortable outdoors. She switched off Pam Taylor's face and took out her art portfolio from one of the drawers in the work-table that stretched down the middle of the room. She began to colour some sketches she'd done of a spray of orchids. It wasn't urgent work, but it soothed her mind.

About half an hour later Donny arrived. He plonked an untidy parcel on the table.

'Are you all right?' he asked. 'Are you still miserable about being in the papers? Are you afraid the journalists will track you down, like a celebrity?'

Donny knew, of course. Mum and Dad had said it was Tay's choice, and he didn't have to be told, but she couldn't have imagined keeping a secret like that from him.

'Nah,' said Tay. 'The Lifeforce Teenage Clone Protection Programme will look after me. I'm like someone giving evidence against the Mob. The newspapers and TV will never find me . . . Is that the frog?'

'Yes.' He unwrapped his parcel, revealing a splendid tree-frog, standing on its back legs. It was varnished in red and green, and fixed to a bamboo stand. There was a perpetual calendar fitted into the frog's belly, and it had a wide, gaping mouth for holding letters. One of the frog's back feet was missing.

'I've got her foot. But the clamp I made for holding the letters has come unsprung.'

'Right,' said Tay. 'The doctor is in.'

They fixed the frog (as well as could be expected, for a papier-mâché model that had spent time knocking around in an aeroplane hold with Donny's socks). Then they checked the status of Mum's big present: which was a dozen Old English rose bushes, specially genetically adapted for the tropics, that Tay had ordered on the internet (she'd got Dad to do the ordering on his credit card, and promised to pay him back).

The bushes wouldn't look like much *now*, but there would be pictures of how the flowers were going to look: and Mum would love them. She was the one with the green fingers, who was responsible for the success of all the flowerbeds in the Refuge clearing. The roses were due to arrive with the next mail drop. Donny and Tay would have to make sure they got to the mail parcel (however it reached the Refuge) before their mother.

'If they don't come because of the rebels,' said Donny, cheerfully, 'at least she's got my frog. It can be from both of us if you like.'

'Thanks. Did you buy her a card?'

'I thought I'd make one. She likes home-made things.'

'Me too. Let's get to it. Then it'll be done and we'll be all set.'

The schoolroom grew busy and cosy and quiet: the two children working together, tearing up coloured tissue paper, passing the glue, asking for the scissors, like long ago. In two years, thought Tay, I'll be sixteen. I'll be old enough to go away to college, and then I'll face my destiny. People will find out I'm a clone, but I won't mind. I will be the second Pam Taylor. I will be a brilliant success. Mum and Dad won't have to blame themselves for how they had me, and everything will turn out well. But I'm not going to think about it until then. Until then I'm just going to be Tay.

When they'd finished the cards they left them to dry and went over to the observation studio. The baby apes spent all their time with their carers, the way orang-utan babies live alone with their mothers in the wild. The older apes had an enclosure on the edge of the clearing, so they could start learning to forage and look after themselves. They also had a suite of indoor pens, which the Refuge staff called the 'clubhouse', where they were free to come and go, and socialise with each other – and where the scientists could observe their behaviour on CCTV.

Sometimes there was a proper experiment. One of the visiting primatologists (people who study apes), or the graduate students, might be observing how the apes solved a puzzle. But there was always *something* going on, and usually (even though everything was being videoed) one of the scientists would be watching. Today they found Dr Suritobo, the Refuge's animal psychologist, on his own in front of the monitor screens – like a security guard watching some very hairy teenagers hanging out in a shopping mall.

'Hi, Clint,' said Tay. 'What's up?'

Dr Suritobo was Indonesian. He'd been with Lifeforce as long as Mum and Dad had, and he'd written a shelf-full of books, but he never seemed entirely like a grown-up. He could make bows and arrows that really worked; and strange musical instruments out of bamboo. He was the best guide for jungle walks, too. No one called him anything but Clint, because he was a fanatical Clint Eastwood fan. He even had a poncho (a striped, hand-woven, Dyak poncho; but it looked the part). You'd find him loping around with his hat brim pulled down over his narrowed eyes, chewing on a thin black cheroot, obviously deep in some *The Good, The Bad And The Ugly* fantasy. The children loved him, though they sometimes wondered how he managed to hold down a responsible job.

But Clint had told them there should be no difference between work and play, anyway.

He was pleased to see them. He stretched his arms above his head, and ran his hands through his hair, which was already standing on end.

'Hi! Always something new on orang-utan TV! Sit down! Bring on the popcorn.'

Five 'teenage' orang-utans, nearly ready to be introduced back to the wild, were sitting together in the section of the 'clubhouse' that had a climbing gym of tree branches, ropes and swings (like a sofa and armchairs to orang-utans, Tay thought). An ape called Potter was up in the tree, looking defiant. Genevieve was there, off by herself. Bima, the most 'dominant' of the adolescents, was sitting with two younger apes, known as Juju and Henry: they were hunched up close together, obviously miserable and sulking.

Tay had no trouble recognising the apes. The human children weren't allowed near the babies, and they were supposed to keep away from the older apes (though they could sometimes earn pocket money cleaning out the club-house). It was very important that the animals didn't get used to humans: they weren't pets. But Donny and Tay had watched a huge amount of 'orang-utan TV'. It was their favourite entertainment.

'They're not doing anything much,' said Donny, after a few minutes.

'Yes they are, Donny,' said Clint. 'This is a serious con-versation. *Watch!*'

Orang-utans, unlike gibbons, are mainly silent animals. The 'conversation' was wordless. Genevieve stared at Bima, gave a hard, brooding glare at Potter in the tree, and then flopped down on her side, her head propped on one long-fingered, furry-backed hand, the other hand scratching at her pot-belly.

'Is that, er . . . Juju and Henry under the tree?' asked Donny.

'Yep. Two sad souls. They should lighten up . . . That's what Bima is telling them.'

Donny glowed, proud that he could still name the apes, though he had to go to school.

'What's it all about?' asked Tay. 'What did Potter do to Henry and Juju?'

Clint laughed. 'I have no idea! It must have happened in an episode I missed. But Bima seems to think those two aren't completely innocent.'

Bima wasn't as clever as Potter, or as old as Genevieve, but he was big, kind-hearted and fair, and the others looked up to him because he settled arguments. At that moment the ape called Potter – who had bright small eyes, and a naturally wicked expression on his long-lipped, fur-framed face – leaned out and carefully spit a melon seed right onto the red, shaggy head of one of the sulking pair. Donny and Tay laughed.

'You see?' said Clint. 'The pip-spitting is very insulting, almost fighting talk and, as we know, Bima doesn't let the others fight; but Bima hasn't told Potter off—'

'Don't you ever wish you could just *ask* them what's going on?' wondered Tay. 'I bet Potter and Bima are clever enough to learn sign language; and Genevieve.'

Clint shook his head. 'Maybe, but that's not our job. Already these young apes have been changed too much. They have been stolen from their mothers to be sold as pets, or orphaned when their mothers were killed by human activity, in one way or another. They have learned to depend on each other for company, which would never happen in the wild. They should be solitary creatures, and they will become solitary again, if we can return them to the forest . . . No, Tay, I don't want them to learn to "talk" to me, like fake human beings. I want them to be orang-utans.'

'Why did you say "if"?' asked Tay, picking on this word uneasily. 'Of course we're going to release them.'

'Of course,' said Clint, with a sigh. 'Of course, yes, for a while longer. We have the Sultan of Kandah on our side. But who knows what the future will bring?'

'If the rebels win, do you think they'll want to close us down?' Donny wondered.

'Ha! I don't think they will ever agree on what they want. But with luck, thank God, none of those outlaw bands is going to "win". They'll just back down again—'

The door of the studio opened and an orang-utan ambled in. Unlike the apes on the screen, he was an adult: and he was different in other ways. If you knew anything about orang-utans the shape of his cheek-jowls told you at once that he came from Sumatra, not Borneo. This was Uncle, the Refuge's mascot. Uncle had been sent to the Lifeforce Refuge when one of the last orang-utan rehabilitation centres in Sumatra had to close down. The staff there had tried and failed to return him to the forest: Uncle had just kept coming back to them. Now it didn't matter if he spent his time with humans, and it didn't matter that he didn't belong in Borneo, because he was too old to be released. He had the run of the compound, but Clint was his special friend.

Uncle pushed out his lip to the children in greeting and stood, knuckling the ground with one hand while he scratched his throat with the other. He gazed severely at Clint.

'Ah! My secretary!' exclaimed Clint. 'It must be time for the team meeting.'

He glanced at Tay. 'Donny, will you go and tell your mum and dad and the others I'll be there in a few minutes? I want to show Tay how to continue noting this inter-action—'

'Sure thing, pardner.'

Donny left. Clint put his laptop in front of Tay. 'Excuse an old friend, my dear girl, but I've heard rumours that you may be having a tough time right about now?'

'I'm okay.'

'Uh-huh,' Clint leaned back, and tipped the brim of an imaginary hat over his eyes. 'You know, Tay, I think you have to ask yourself one question about all this.'

'Oh, yeah?'

She didn't want to talk about it, but there was something in his tone that was new—

'You want to be a scientist, I do believe. You want to be out at the edge of human knowledge, making the first foot-prints into the unknown? So, you have to ask yourself this. If someone had made you an offer, all those years ago, that meant you could be part of something risky but very exciting, something wild and strange that had never been tried before – what would you have said?'

'That's two questions.'

'True,' said Clint, smiling but serious. 'You can answer them both.'

'I want to be a *major* scientist,' said Tay. 'And yes. I would probably have said yes.'

Clint nodded. 'I think you would have said yes. Think of that. Remember that.'

Clint went to his meeting. Tay settled down to watch the apes, typing brief notes about what she thought was happening – notes which could be compared, later, with the videotape. No one could ask me, she thought. It was an amazing thing to be able to do, and they couldn't ask me whether I would agree to be part of it. Parents can never ask their children if they want to be born, not even ordinary children. No one lied to me. They told me as much as I could understand, from the moment I was old enough to listen. They've been as fair as they could possibly be.

But it's strange how the more they tell me I'm special, the more I feel like an orphan.

Bima went over to the sofa (that is, to the branches) and shook them, gazing up at Potter. Potter gave a resigned 'nnh' grunt and swung himself to the ground. Genevieve immediately cheered up, and ambled over. Bima was making Potter and Juju hold hands. *Let's not fight*, thought Tay, imagining the dialogue. *We've only got each other*. Me and the apes, she thought. We're in the same fix. But they can be returned to the wild, where they belong, and I can't. Clones don't have a natural habitat.

Hey, she told herself. *Stop thinking about it*!

Uncle had stayed behind when Clint left. He sat in another chair, two places away from Tay along the observation desk, with his feet up, watching Tay out of the corner of his eye. Uncle weighed about a hundred and sixty pounds. His shambling body was full of muscle and his massive jaws were equipped with big teeth. He could have made a formidable predator, if that had been his nature. But it never crossed anyone's mind to be afraid of him. He reached out with one of his long shaggy arms, and gently patted her shoulder. Tay looked around, and smiled.

'Thanks, Uncle. *You* understand. I know you do.'

*

28

Things that you've planned for and imagined rarely turn out as good as you expected, but Mum's birthday was an exception. Genevieve had been safely delivered to Half-Way Camp, and the children had spent two blissful nights up there with Dad, camping in the wild. A successful release always put everyone in a good mood; the rebel situation had calmed down, and the rose bushes had arrived safely.

Tessa Mahakam, the head of the ape veterinary team, woke people up before dawn, and they went out into the forest on foot, to an outcrop where they could climb up and watch the sunrise. Tessa was a Dyak. She'd been to university in America, and spent years there; but she'd been a little girl in the Kandah highlands, when the older people still remembered a time when the tribe had had no idea that modern civilisation existed. Greeting the dawn was a tradition from her childhood, which the Refuge had adopted for special occasions. Thirty-five grown-up humans, two children and one adult orang-utan stood above a sea of trees and watched the light change, until the red-gold globe had risen safely, once more, into the blossoming sky. They cheered and clapped and stamped, and marched back home, singing '*By the Rivers of Babylon*', loudly and quite tunefully. (It was one of Mum's favourite songs.)

The baby-ape carers had to leave. Everybody who could stay stayed for a special breakfast. There was ripe papaya with lime, scrambled eggs, bacon (for the non-Muslims), chilled chocolate milk, sweet bread with sticky coconut inside, and Java coffee for the grown-ups. There was one of Minah's magnificent cakes on display (to be eaten later). It had green and yellow icing, and an orang-utan made of sugar-paste, holding up a sign that said 'Happy Birthday To Our Chief' in tiny letters. Then there were the presents, including the rose bushes: a beautiful gold-thread hand-woven silk sarong from Dad, and a rare obscure book about orang-utan research from the shy German zoologist. Tessa took down Mum's long black hair, combed it out and arranged it with the antique beaded headband that was *her* present, and some glowing white frangipani flowers. Mum modelled the new sarong – without taking off her shorts, but you could get the idea.

It was a perfect day; and a perfect evening later, with a party meal and a movie.

Unfortunately, the good news didn't last. Two days after the birthday celebrations they heard by radio that all the movement restrictions were in force again. Donny and Tay came into the bungalow kitchen at lunchtime, and overheard Mum and Dad talking in low voices about 'sending the children to Singapore'.

They sneaked out before they were noticed, and retired to a thorny-palm thicket at the far end of the clearing, beyond the teenage ape enclosure, where they knew they wouldn't be disturbed. It was the middle of a very hot day, and a quivering hush had fallen, like a cloud, over the whole clearing. Even the gibbons were quiet.

'I can't believe it,' whispered Donny, outraged. 'If it's dangerous, how could we want to be out of danger, *leaving Mum and Dad behind*?'

'Maybe it will blow over,' said Tay. But being sent back to Singapore in the middle of the holidays was an awful threat. The trouble must be getting serious.

She was thinking that this stillness felt like the moment before a thunderstorm. When the Walkers had moved to Kandah there'd been thunderstorms nearly every day, all the year round. Though summer was called the dry season, you'd hardly been able to tell it from the slightly-more-wet winter. But for the last few summers there'd been drought conditions. It was a problem, because of the risk of fires.

'If they tell us we have to go,' she said, 'we'll argue our case. We must be prepared.'

'Right. Let's think of things to say, to convince them we don't have to leave.'

Before they could come up with anything, they heard a strange, sharp ringing sound, with an echo. And another—

Crack . . . *zing*—

'That sounds like a gun!' exclaimed Donny.

It *was* a gun. When they looked out from the thicket they saw Clint, wearing his treasured black cowboy hat and his Dyak poncho, leaping about in the secluded space between the Land Rover garage and the perimeter fence. Uncle was there too. Clint had set up a row of cans on a fallen tree trunk. He was firing at them with a long-barrelled pistol: then gathering up the ones he'd hit and starting again. The children approached, fascinated. There were shotguns at the Refuge. Tay knew how to use one: Donny would be taught too, now that he was twelve. But they were kept locked up.

'What are you doing?' said Tay, when they were close enough. 'Is that a real gun?'

'Yep, it's real,' said Dr Suritobo, tipping the brim of his hat with the barrel of the pistol, like the man with no name. He reloaded, and spun around.

Wham! Wham, wham, wham, wham, wham!

Uncle put his hands over his ears. Two cans went down, another wobbled but stayed upright. 'Hm. I need to practise.'

'Where did you get it from? Why are you doing this?'

'Because I'm Indonesian. A crazy Indonesian rainforest cowpuncher, pardners.'

Tay wrapped her arms around herself, suddenly chilled.

31

'You mean because you're a foreigner?' said Donny. 'Do you think the rebels will come and kill you? Oh, wow. Do you think they'll kill us, too?'

Clint blew away cordite smoke, and shook his head.

'I think nothing will happen. Don't tell your mother about my target practice.'

'I expect she knows,' said Tay.

There wasn't much that went on at the Refuge that Mum didn't know about.

'Do you know why Uncle wouldn't let them return him to the forest?' said Clint. 'It's because he knows it's over. In a few years there will be no orang-utans left except in zoos. You know it, don't you, Uncle? But we'll fight to the last.'

'Don't say that!' cried Tay. 'There's hundreds and thousands of miles of forest still. The apes can have a share. Why can't human people ever *share*?'

Clint started to reload his big old-fashioned handgun; and suddenly the rain came down, with a hiss and a roar. The children were drenched in seconds, gouts of white, shining water streaming from their T-shirts and shorts. Uncle, his fur equally streaming, ambled over to replace the cans, and then stood there with his arms around his head, peering out at the children from between his elbow and his forearm.

Ordinarily Donny and Tay would have enjoyed the rain. But suddenly there was no fun in getting drenched. They went indoors to change their clothes, leaving the ape and Dr Suritobo to their ominous game.

Two

A week went by and nothing happened, except that once more there was no mail drop. Only army planes and helicopters were allowed to fly over the forest. The Refuge staff prepared for the worst – contacting other Refuges, and even zoos, and generally working out how they would cope if they had to evacuate the apes in a hurry. But they meant to hold on. 'Possession is nine-tenths of the law,' said Dad. 'If we leave because of a temporary crisis, we might lose the reserve forever.'

Nothing more was said about sending Tay and Donny to Singapore. On Friday, a week and a half after Mum's birthday, Tay asked if they could go out by themselves for a whole day's adventure. Mum agreed, on the usual conditions. Take survival kit and a radiophone. Leave an itinerary posted on the common-room noticeboard. That means you say who you are, where you're going and when you expect to be back, and you *don't* change your minds and go somewhere else once you're out in the forest. Phone in if you are going to be late, and don't be out after dark, for anything less than a real emergency.

'Obey these sacred instructions,' said Mum, as she always did. 'And all will be well. If you break any of the rules, and I find out, *you are grounded for life.*'

'Yes Ma'am!' said Tay, saluting smartly. The clone business was buried; they just weren't going to talk about it for a while. It was bad news about the rebels, but great to be back to normal; to be Mum and Tay again.

On Saturday, Tay woke Donny early, to the gibbons' dawn chorus. It was the children's job to help Minah the cook on Saturdays (which they didn't mind; it was a good way to influence the Saturday night menu). Before seven o'clock, Tay and Donny had eaten their breakfast and were busy cleaning pans, fetching rice and beans from the storage loft in the kitchen roof, and scraping fresh coconut for the creamy, sticky pudding called gula malacca, their favourite dessert. By eight-thirty, they were free.

Mum wasn't around. She was in the ape clinic checking on an orphan baby who'd been taken ill in the night. Dad was in the staff common room, on the main square, holding a noisy vote for the Saturday night movie. Traditionally it would be something ancient and cheesy: *Gremlins Two* was a favourite, and so was *Jurassic Park*. Dr Suritobo was trying to hustle another showing of the greatest movie ever made (which meant, naturally, *The Good, The Bad And The Ugly*), but he was being shouted down. Tay pinned her notice to the board, ignoring the rowdy scientists. It was very simple. It read: *We're going to the caves, we'll be back before dark. Donny and Tay.*

Dad nodded and waved, and went on with his vote counting.

The caves were in the rocky outcrop where they'd watched the sun rise on Mum's birthday: Clint and Tessa had discovered them. The Refuge staff (those who liked being underground, at least) had been investigating the maze of caverns gradually. In the wet season there wasn't much to see because the passages were flooded, but every dry season there was more that could be explored.

34

It would be hot already out in the open, but the morning was cool under the shelter of the great trees. Donny and Tay walked silently, following the familiar red earth path. Far above, the sky in the gaps in the forest canopy was a clear and vivid blue. Butterflies flitted by. A jungle pigeon called like a chiming bell: a hornbill crossed from tree to tree, its huge yellow bill looking twice the size of the bird. Flowers shone like jewels in the deep green shadows on either side.

If they were very quiet and very lucky, they might see a mouse-deer.

In the forest, thought Tay, it doesn't matter what I am. I am the newest thing on earth, walking among the ancient guardians of life. Everything that makes me strange and weird vanishes into their silence. Oh, I hope we don't have to leave . . .

TV reception at the Refuge was never any good, and they often had trouble getting connected to the internet; but they could listen to the radio. Last night the news had sounded a little better. The Sultan was negotiating with the army of rebels who had advanced into the Kandah River Region (which included both Kandah City and the orang-utan reserve).

'What does it mean when they say the Sultan's "negotiating"?' asked Donny.

'It means he's trying to bargain. You know, like in the market. The rebels say, we want *this much* before we'll go away . . . and the Sultan rolls his eyes and pretends that's impossible, and then the rebels offer a slightly lower price—'

'Eh! *Tak' bisa!*' cried Donny, rolling his eyes. 'It would be an insult to my family—!'

Tak' bisa means *can't do that*. It was what village market women said, whatever you offered them and whatever you were buying. You had to haggle; they'd be offended if you didn't play their game. Donny giggled, pleased with his impression of the Sultan. 'I bet he has to give them a lot of money. Do they take travellers' cheques?'

'I don't think it's money they want . . . Donny, shut up. You said you'd keep quiet. We won't see any wildlife if you're chattering.'

'All right, I'll hoot like a gibbon instead—'

Donny hooted: not much like a gibbon, but horribly loud. Tay broke into a run, to get away from him. Thrilled by her own sure-footed speed, she kept on running until she burst out of the trees; and on and on, upwards into the hot sunshine.

She sat waiting for him on a sunny rock half-way up the outcrop.

'Cheat,' glowered Donny, puffed and sweating. 'You're used to running on rough ground. I'm not. I twisted my foot. That wasn't fair.'

'Excuses, excuses.'

He sat down and cheered up as he watched a trail of fire ants advancing on his left boot. 'It's so *excellent* living here. With killer ants and monster lizards and everything . . . I want to stay in the forest forever.'

'Me too. Come on. We should be able to get past the flooded bit easily, and then I've got some ideas for new places to explore—'

Donny was the first to wriggle through the cleft in the rocks. As she was about to follow him, Tay saw a patch of rust-red fur moving on the steep slope beneath her. It was an orang-utan, and she knew it must be Uncle. The release areas for the orphans were nowhere near here, and no wild ape would come so near a human. They usually stayed up in the high canopy. Uncle was free to come and go, he had no trouble climbing the perimeter fence; but he rarely ventured outside the clearing. He stopped about twenty metres away, surprisingly well camouflaged against a big red-brown boulder.

'What are you doing here?' called Tay. 'Are you following us?'

Everyone at the Refuge talked to Uncle as if he was human. He seemed to understand a good deal, too, no matter what language you were using. He sat down, folded his arms and looked at the sky, as if he was pretending he'd just come for a stroll.

Donny's head popped out of the cleft.

'What's up?'

'It's Uncle. He's followed us.'

'Does that mean we have to take him back?'

'No,' decided Tay. 'He can look after himself. He's a grown-up.'

She stared at the great red ape, wondering what was going through his mind. He wasn't a pet, he was more like a . . . She couldn't think of a word for it. He was just there. A wild animal who chose not to be wild. Uncle went on pretending not to notice her. Orang-utans have a great ability to do nothing, ignore you, and make you feel an idiot.

'He can look after himself,' she repeated. 'Get out of my way, I'm coming down.'

The next few hours were very interesting. The passage that led to the deeper caves had dried out sufficiently that they could wade the dip. On the other side there was a thrilling larger cave, which they'd only visited once before, with stalactites and stalagmites, and sheets of stone like marble curtains sweeping down from the dark above. The shoots of stone that grew from the floor all made different sounds if you tapped them. They spent ages searching for the sweet spots that resonated best, playing symphonies to the echoes, and sending stone text messages to each other.

Then they went on, into passages that maybe even Tessa and Clint had never seen. They ate their packed lunch – early, because Donny was starving – and wriggled through a crawl-space into a cave full of bats, with stinking bat-dirt thick as a feather-bed on the floor. Donny had visions of making a fortune by selling it for fertiliser. Then there was a gallery where the roof was coated with a gleaming, white, phosphorescent sort of lichen like fringed snowflakes, which Tay photographed with care, hoping it was something unknown to science. There were chasms to be leapt – not wide, but exciting. There were spooky echoes to be sounded. The caves seemed to have no end. The whole outcrop must be riddled with them.

'People would pay loads of dollars to see all this!' gloated Donny.

'Yeah, maybe. But no tourists in the Lifeforce orang-utan reserve, remember?'

'Oh, I forgot. Drat.'

Tay was amazed when she checked her watch and found it was nearly four in the afternoon. Time to turn back. There was no danger of getting lost. They'd been marking the walls with chalk, and Tay was good at keeping maps in her head; but she set a brisk pace. There were places where they would have to wriggle and squirm, and she wanted to be absolutely sure of being home before dark.

It was Donny who first noticed something wrong.

'Tay?' he said. 'Can you smell smoke?'

As soon as he said it, the smell was unmistakable.

The children stopped dead, the light from their headband lamps painting hollow shadows on their dirty faces. Fear. The fear was immediate.

'It could be a little brush fire on the outcrop,' said Tay. 'It could be nothing much.'

They didn't panic, but they'd lived long enough in the wilderness to know how quickly a hint of danger can turn into real trouble. They hurried on, saying hardly a word to each other. At the longest crawl-space, where they had to get down on their hands and knees, the smell of smoke was stronger, but neither of them mentioned this. Through the crawl-space, and they were back in the big cavern with the stalactites. Here the smoke was visible. They could see little winding trails of it, wreathing around in their headlamp beams, in the darkness overhead.

They looked at each other, trying not to feel afraid—

'We'll be okay in the entrance cave,' said Tay. 'Smoke's getting through cracks in rock down here, but the entrance cave is higher, it should be clear.'

They waded through the dip in the passage, and now they could hear the fire: like the muffled buzzing of a swarm of insects, like a humming, rustling thunder. The entrance cave was not clear; it was hazed with smoke. Red-tinged daylight flickered, from the cleft where they had slithered in. Suddenly something dark loomed between the children and the light.

They both yelled in shock: but it was Uncle!

'What are you doing in here?' demanded Tay. 'Apes don't live underground.'

Uncle grabbed onto the children with his long arms, and hugged them. Tay could feel his heart beating hard, under his shaggy fur. He was frightened too.

'We can't get out!' gasped Donny. 'It's a real fire! What are we going to do?'

'Well, the first thing is call and tell Mum and Dad.'

That was when they discovered that the radiophone wouldn't work.

'Does the battery need charging? You should have checked it, Tay.'

'There's nothing wrong with the battery. It's because we're underground.' Tay thought hard. 'Donny, this is what we'll do. We're perfectly safe. We'll wait in here until the fire dies down. Mum and Dad know where we are. They'll send help if this goes on . . . but they've probably got enough on their hands at the moment.'

She thought of fire sweeping through the Refuge clearing. Donny must be thinking the same thing, but he didn't say so. It wasn't going to make them feel better.

'What about the smoke? We shouldn't be breathing smoke, should we?'

'Take off your lamp, and your T-shirt.'

Tay took off her helmet, shucked her rucksack from her shoulders and pulled her own shirt over her head. 'We'll soak them in the dip in the passage, and hold them over our faces. I think we should stay near the entrance in case Mum and Dad come. The heat and smoke won't get worse here, because there's nothing much to burn outside.'

Tay was wearing a cotton scarf around her neck, like a cowboy bandana. She soaked this as well as her T-shirt, and gave it to the ape. Uncle picked up what it was for at once. At the back of the cave they found a place where they could climb over a natural barrier wall into a small, sheltered hollow. Uncle climbed as if he was in a tree, helped the children over with his long arms, and at once they could breathe more easily.

They switched off their lamps. The fire outside was giving some light, and there was nothing much to see, anyway. Uncle set himself on the outside of the hollow, between the

40

children and the sheet of rock that hid the main cave. He had wrapped Tay's scarf around his face. Every few seconds he'd lower it to peep out, and check, as if counting his charges . . . One, two. Two children, still there, still safe.

'He's like that dog in *Peter Pan*,' said Donny, with a shaky laugh. 'The one that's a nursemaid. He's looking after us.'

The fire roared on.

Donny shifted his damp T-shirt to say, 'We're not going to be back by dark.'

'No, but we haven't broken any rules. Are you hungry?'

They had spare food, and spare lights.

'No.'

When Tay climbed out (scraping her ribs, and feeling like a skinned rabbit in just her shorts and bra) to wet the shirts and her scarf again, the floor of the entrance cave was covered in crawling things: beetles and millipedes and stranger creatures. Bigger animals, maybe rats and mice, or snakes and lizards, moved in the shadows. She tried not to step on anything that was alive. They weren't hungry, but they drank some bottled water (Uncle sipped from their water bottle; he knew how to do that). At last, after several hours, the sound of the flames faded, and the air cleared. But by now it was completely dark. Tay clambered out with the phone, and stood under the cleft. She couldn't climb up, the rock was too hot to touch.

No answer. No response at all.

In Kandah, ordinary mobile phones only worked on the coastal strip, where the city was, and a few other biggish towns. The Refuge radiophones had a limited range. For anything more than talking to each other within a few kilometres, the staff used their satellite connection. But the phone ought to be working here, and no matter what they

41

were doing, someone should answer. She ought to be getting *something* . . .

'I think we'll have to stay overnight,' she said, when she got back. 'It's too hot out there, we'll have to wait until the ground cools down.'

'What did Mum and Dad say?'

'I can't get through. I think the battery's dead.'

'You should have checked it. We're always supposed to do that.'

'Yes,' said Tay. 'I should have checked it.' The radiophone battery was not the problem, it was fine. But she couldn't bear to tell him that, not yet. 'I expect they tried to call us and they couldn't get through. They're trusting us to be sensible.'

'Yeah,' said Donny. 'They'll be here in the morning.'

And so they spent the night. There was no space to lie down, but neither of them wanted to get out and lie on the cave floor among the creepy-crawlies. Donny managed to fall asleep. Tay sat with her arm around him, full of fears that she dared not put into words, not even in her own mind. She felt a tugging at her wrist. The great ape took her hand, and squeezed it; and that was a comfort.

Donny was bewildered. He hadn't figured it out. But Uncle always knew things.

At first light, Tay woke from a confused doze. She woke Donny: Uncle was already awake. The cave was full of dull daylight and empty of wildlife. All the other refugees had left the shelter. 'You two stay here,' she said. 'I'll see what it's like outside.'

Feeling sick and scared, she climbed the chute that led to the cleft. The loose stones were hot under her hands and knees, but not hot enough to burn her.

The outcrop had been covered in scrubby, orange-flowering bushes, the kind that the butterflies loved. Lower down there'd been graceful stands of bamboo, and thorny pandanus palm. Everything was gone. There wasn't a scrap of green on the slopes. The blackened skeletons of the butterfly bushes reached out twisted dead fingers over grey ash and baked stone. The path seemed to have disappeared, because there was no undergrowth to mark the difference between path and scrub. The smoke had cleared, but there was no freshness in the morning. The sky was grey as ash, and the sultry air smelled foul. She tried the phone again, without much hope, and got the same result.

But below her, the trees were standing. The red-brown trunks were burned charcoal black, and the low branches were smouldering, all around the outcrop. But the fire had passed by, and the trees were standing! And the high canopy was still green.

Her spirits rose a little. 'It's okay!' she called. 'It's over, and the damage doesn't look terrible. Something's wrong with the phone, but I think we're going to be all right.'

The great ape clambered out first, and then Donny. The three of them stared at a devastated landscape. It was hard to believe that, twenty-four hours ago, everything had been normal. Uncle hopped from foot to foot. He touched the ground with one of his big, graceful hands and brought his fingers back to his mouth, making a long lip to kiss them several times: Ouch, ouch.

'He can't walk on this,' said Tay. 'What can we do with him? We have to get back.'

'I k-know,' said Donny. His teeth were chattering, not from cold but from the strain of the night. 'We can t-tear up my T-shirt, to make shoes he can wear.'

They didn't tear up Donny's T-shirt; Tay thought that

43

was a bad idea, but they managed to make Uncle a pair of snowshoes (or fireshoes). Donny's rucksack became one shoe – after they'd stuffed everything that was in it into Tay's bag. Their notebook, which luckily had a board cover, made the other. They tied it to his foot with the plastic bag that had held their biscuits. Uncle sat patiently on Tay's rucksack while the children fitted these odd slippers on to his long-fingered feet.

'Maybe you'll start a fashion,' said Donny. Uncle looked disgusted, but grateful.

They followed the path, which was clear underfoot although invisible from a distance. If you stepped off it you raised clouds of hot, choking ash. Even on the path they could feel the heat through the soles of their boots. It was better once they were among the trees; except for the smouldering branches that had fallen on the path. They got along as best they could. Uncle struggled with his ridiculous footwear (but they didn't feel like laughing). Tay wanted to hurry, she wanted to run: but at the same time she could hardly make herself put one foot in front of the other . . .

Everyone must have been fighting the fire all night. Everyone must be exhausted. That must be why no one had come to find them—

She didn't try to use the radiophone again.

They reached the jeep track, and then the perimeter fence. The gates were wide open and leaning, warped out of shape. The fire had been through the Refuge clearing. Most of the buildings were standing: charred black, like the scrub bushes on the outcrop, like the trunks of the trees. But there was nothing moving. No sign of life.

'Mum!' cried Donny, his voice breaking. 'Mum and Dad!'

44

'It's all right Donny, it's all right. It looks bad but they won't be—'

They won't be dead. Mum and Dad can't be *dead*.

Slowly, very slowly, as if they were blindfold, or sleepwalking, they walked into what had been their home. There were no flowerbeds. Some of the beautiful trees were still sullenly burning, with flames and smoke instead of flowers in their branches. Smoke and ash hung in the air, and everything seemed *wrong*. It was as if they'd landed on an alien planet. Tay couldn't get her bearings. Where were the staff cottages? Was that the generator house . . . ? Where had the helicopter pad gone? What had happened to the clubhouse?

She picked up a charred book which was lying on the ground in a spray of shattered glass. It was a copy of Shakespeare, a pocket edition that Tay and Donny's gran had sent to Tay for Christmas, two years ago. She'd never even tried to read it, the print was too small. She was standing under her own bedroom window. The book must have been on the windowsill; it must have been blown out when her window was shattered by the heat. She stuffed it in the pocket of her rucksack, from a confused feeling that she must salvage things. All my clothes will be ruined, she thought. Suddenly she spun around, hunting for a familiar outline. The bamboo stand where the gibbons lived had vanished.

'Oh, no,' she whispered. The numbness of terrible fear released her, and tears stung her eyes. They are gone, they are gone. They won't sing their dawn chorus ever again.

'Where *is* everybody?' said Donny, in a small, thin voice.

Inside the central square, something different had happened. There were churned-up vehicle tracks everywhere, showing through the ash. The bungalow was scarred by fire like the rest of the buildings: but on the other side of the open space, where the observation studio and telecoms suite, with its big dish aerial ought to be, there was only wreckage around a gaping hole, like a meteor crater.

'The fire didn't do that—' muttered Tay, staring.

Uncle had found something. He was crouched down, making anxious 'nnh!' noises. Tay went over to see what was wrong. There was a burned body lying on the ground.

She knelt, feeling very dizzy and strange, and forced herself to turn the body over. It was Lucia Fernandez. Tay knew her by the locket she always wore, which the fire hadn't touched. She was dead. She was burned black. But how, why? Why hadn't she run from the fire? Unless she had died some other way, and the fire had burned her afterwards . . . Tay tried to think clearly. She knew she must think, work this out, decide what to do. But here was someone she knew, *dead*. She couldn't take it in. In her mind she heard Lucia's teasing voice, at the airport, saying: *You two, you jabber like monkeys—*

She stood up.

'MUM!' she shouted. 'DAD! Please! Where are you?'

No answer.

Donny came and stood beside her, looking down. He clutched her hand. 'Shouldn't we say something?' he whispered, as if Lucia were asleep and he might wake her. 'We ought to say a prayer. That's what people do, isn't it? When someone's dead?'

'Okay, I'll try. Please God . . .' But nothing more would come, no words.

They just stood there.

'Donny,' said Tay, at last. 'The rebels did this.'

'Yeah. I think so too.'

'Look at all these tracks. The rebels came here, they killed

Lucia, they started the fire. I think they must have taken everybody else away.'

'M-Mum and Dad and everybody's been kidnapped? Oh Tay, what'll we do?'

'I'm thinking.' She felt the faintest glimmer of hope. The rebels must have come to loot the Refuge, and taken the staff away hoping that Lifeforce would pay a ransom.

'We have to get help, Donny. We have to tell someone what's happened, but our phone doesn't work and the ground station is wrecked. We'll have to get to Kandah City.'

'Yes. We'll have to do that. But how?'

'I'm not sure. We'll walk out to the main road. Maybe we can get a lift . . . Look, whatever we decide to do, we'll need supplies. Let's go to the kitchen and see if any food stores survived. And water. We'll need water.'

Donny nodded, relieved to have something to do. 'All right.'

'We'll get help, Donny. Everyone's depending on us. We can do this.'

If she told herself that often enough, maybe it would come true.

The kitchen house was the oldest building in the clearing. It was traditional-built, like the Walkers' home bungalow, with a high-ridged roof and massive double-timber walls for coolness, raised on stilts above the ground. The fire had seemed to have swept over and round it, leaving it almost intact. The steps to the doorway, beside the blackened lumps that had been Minah's hen coops, were charred, but not broken.

The electric light wasn't working, and the windows were so blackened by smoke that they had to switch on their torches, which they'd been carrying to back up their head-lamps. The food in the big fridge and in the freezers was spoiled. Even some of the plastic utensils hanging on the walls had flowed into strange shapes. But the larder door had been shut, and the dry stores in there were safe. They found a bigger rucksack on a shelf, and began sorting things to pack, and discarding non-essentials like Tay's camera and their caving helmets.

'As much water as we can both carry. Food too, because we might be stranded for days, but we must have plenty of water—' said Tay. It was a long way to Kandah City if they had to walk, and the fire might be in their path. They might have to detour through the forest, and they'd better avoid the villages because—

Suddenly Donny grabbed her.

They stared upwards. They'd both heard something move, up in the storage loft.

'Who's there?' shouted Tay. No answer.

The loft ladder was lying on the floor. It was big and heavy, but they managed to get it into place. 'You stay here,' whispered Tay. 'I'll go up.'

'What, *unarmed?*' breathed Donny.

They looked around for weapons. But Uncle, who had followed them into the kitchen, silently pushed them aside, grabbed the ladder and was in the loft in a couple of swings. They heard him make an eager sound of welcome.

'It's Clint!' gasped Tay. 'Oh it's *Clint*! That's his Clint noise!'

The children rushed up the ladder. In the half-dark, between the sacks of rice and stacks of cardboard boxes, they saw Uncle crouched beside someone who was sitting propped against the wall. They shone their torches. Clint didn't get up or speak as they came over. His face and hands were scorched black, and the left leg of his trousers was glistening with something Tay guessed must be blood.

48

'Howdy, pardners,' he said, when they were near him. 'I've been waiting for you.'

'What happened?' demanded Donny.

'Ah, what happened . . . Let me . . .' He pushed himself further upright, grimaced, and closed his eyes, muttering in Indonesian – a version of Malay which the children couldn't understand, unless he was talking slowly.

He opened his eyes again. 'Do you have some water?'

'Yes,' said Tay, ashamed she hadn't thought of it. She knelt, and gave him her water bottle. Clint sipped very carefully, as if he was afraid this one drink might be his last.

'What's wrong with your leg?' asked Donny. 'It's bleeding badly!'

'Bullet wound. It's not bad, Donny, just a graze. A spent bullet grazed me. Well . . . What happened? It's a tale soon told. Yesterday, about noon . . . They came, in a fleet of jeeps. No warning. They said they were going to kill the apes. They want all foreigners out of their country. It's very simple. No apes, no reserve, no reserve means no foreigners here. That's how they saw it. So, ooh, then it was showdown at the OK Corral.'

'You *fought* them,' exclaimed Donny. 'Wow! Like in a war!'

Clint choked on a gasp of bitter laughter. 'We tried to fight them, Donny. It was a very little war . . . Crazy, and hopeless, but we tried.'

'We didn't know,' said Tay. 'We were underground. We only knew about the fire—'

'There was nothing you could have done. You were better where you were. We said we wouldn't let them kill the apes. Some of us scuffled with the outlaws, the rest went to release the apes, and chase them away into the forest. We didn't get out the guns. We thought that would make things worse.

49

We didn't believe the men would actually shoot to kill. But they . . . they shot Lucia . . . to show they meant business. Your mum and dad made a break for it and reached the telecoms suite. They locked themselves in there, to call for help. I don't know if they got through, before the mortar bomb—'

He stopped. He realised what he had said. Tay stared at him, with a ringing in her ears and her heart beating so hard she couldn't catch her breath. Mum is dead. Dad is dead.

'What's a mortar bomb?' asked Donny, and Tay could see he hadn't understood.

'Just a kind of bomb,' said Tay. 'It doesn't matter. Go on, Clint.'

'Well, that's it. The rebels had set the fire, and it was coming. The apes were free, and we can hope some of them have survived. They had the same chance as any other animal out there. But all our people were rounded up, at gunpoint . . . I'd got away when the firing started; I was fetching some vital papers from my house. I heard the explosion in the coms suite. I ran back here, and something hit me. I fell, hit my head. When I came to, everyone was gone, and the fire was coming fast—'

'They took everyone away,' said Donny. 'But everyone but Lucia is okay.'

The look that passed between Tay and Clint said: Donny doesn't have to know.

It might not be true. He doesn't have to be told what might not be true, not right now.

'Reckon you're right there, pardner. I managed to crawl up the loft ladder, before I passed out again. I was here when the fire hit the clearing.'

'Like us in the caves,' said Tay.

'Yeah.' He hugged them, one child with each arm. 'It all

happened so fast. When we knew we were in trouble, there wasn't much time to talk. But I promised Ben and Mary that I would look after you two if I could. And here you are, safe. God is good.'

He let them go, looked at Uncle, and said something in Indonesian. Then the scientist and the great ape hugged each other, and it was strangely as if Uncle was comforting Clint. He stroked his human friend's hair, which was not glossy black any more but smoke-smeared and clotted with ash. Clint's leg wound didn't look like 'just a graze' to Tay. The floor under him was sticky and dark: he must have lost quite a lot of blood.

'I ought to dress that,' she said. 'We have our first aid.'

'You'd better help me down first.' He started trying to get to his feet. 'Ah, this leg has stiffened up . . . Listen, pardners, we're in a tight place. We can't call for help—'

'We have a radiophone,' said Donny. 'But there's something wrong with it.'

'It wouldn't help us, there's no good guys within range . . . We have to get out of here. I daren't take you to Kandah City. From what our outlaws said, and from the way they were behaving, they've taken over the whole region. I'm going to take you across country, to the coast, to the Marine and Shore.' His brown face looked grey, and there were deep lines around his mouth. He leant against one of the roof beams, sweat standing on his forehead.

'But that's a hundred and fifty kilometres away!' cried Tay.

'Yes. Through forest and across the savannah, where there are no settlements, nothing to attract the rebels. And Pam is there. If your mum and dad got through, if she knows what's happened, she'll be moving heaven and earth . . .

51

We'll set off along the East Road, and meet the Lifeforce cavalry, coming to rescue us.'

Tay swallowed hard. Even at this moment, part of her recoiled. Part of her never wanted to see Pam Taylor again. I am a human photocopy, she thought. Oh my mummy, oh my daddy, you don't even belong to me.

But Clint was right. That's the way it had to be.

'Okay,' she said. 'That's what we'll do. But how? You . . . you can't walk.'

'The fire moved through the clearing very fast. If any of the Land Rovers were in the garage they might have survived. Let's go and look.'

When Donny and Tay and Uncle had helped Clint down the ladder he was nearly fainting, and not capable of going anywhere. Tay gave him some aspirin, and cut away the cloth of his trousers so she could see the wound on his leg. Some cloth was stuck inside the flesh, and blood was thickly seeping through a crusted scab.

'I think there's a bullet inside,' she said. 'I ought to get it out.'

Clint laughed. 'No way, little sister! Not without a bottle of red-eye whisky on hand. Or at least a cheroot. No, tie it up and that'll be enough, until I get to a hospital.'

Really, Clint didn't drink. The nearest he came to red-eye whisky was cherry cola. But Uncle must have understood the word 'cheroot'. He went rummaging, while Tay did her best with the wound, and returned with a pack of cigarettes.

Tay had realised that they must all eat something, so while Clint rested after that painful business she hunted for easy food. She found a bowl of eggs in the back of the larder, which turned out to be hard-boiled when she tried to crack them, some cooked rice, and an ant-proof jar of sugar. Minah's gas hob was still working. She put together rice and eggs, and made coffee. Donny gobbled his food. Clint drank black coffee. Uncle ate a little rice, and sat by Clint, taking a draw on his cigarette turn and turn about, and looking very solemn. Tay had thought she wouldn't be able to eat, but she found she was ravenous. The food, and hot sweet coffee, was so strengthening it made her feel drunk. She felt she could do anything. Save Clint and Donny, go after the rebels, save her parents single-handed—

The hole like a meteor crater, where the telecoms suite had been, rose up in her mind, but she knew . . . she'd better not think about that. It might not be true. Might not be true.

They found a broom for Clint to use as a crutch, and went out into the desolation. The Refuge helicopter had been outdoors, grounded by police order, but standing ready in case of an emergency flight. It was fried. So were the vehicles that had been outside. But the garage was a cement and breeze-block hangar standing on a concrete base, and it had been out of the main path of the fire. The doors were still padlocked. Tay used Clint's keys to open them. Inside they found the Refuge's oldest Land Rover, the same one that had once got a flat tyre out in the forest at midnight, when Dad had been 'run over' by a monitor lizard. It was dirty and anonymous: it had no Lifeforce logos on it. Nobody had used it outside the clearing for a long time. But it was functional. Dad had let Tay try out her driving skills in it only a few days ago.

Clint limped up and peered inside, while the children waited anxiously.

'We're in business, pardners. The keys are in the ignition, and I know the tank is full. One thing though.' He turned, leaning heavily on the broomhead crutch under his arm, and held up his scorched hands. 'You'll have to drive, Tay.'

53

Tay nodded. She could tell that for all his brave, cheerful words, Clint was near to collapse. He had seen people he loved either killed or taken off to an unknown fate. He had seen his apes run away into the path of a forest fire, and she was afraid he was in serious pain. She was silently pleading with him to hang on. She could do *anything*: drive a Land Rover, survive in the burned forest, fire a gun. But she had to have someone to tell her what to do. If she had to think, then she would have to think about Lucia. She would have to think about Mum and Dad . . . and she would be lost.

'Fire is like this,' said Clint, patting the old Land Rover. 'It will burn one side of a stream, and not the other. It will burn the house, but not the foundations. It will leap from tree to tree so that only the dead wood dies, and the forest only grows stronger. You must remember that, Tay. *The forest only grows stronger.*'

'Yes,' said Tay, biting her lip. She mustn't cry. 'I'll remember.'

'Food,' muttered Clint: suddenly swaying and almost falling. 'We need food, water—'

Tay got on one side of him. 'Donny!' she yelled. But Uncle was there first, taking Clint's weight. Together the girl and the ape managed to get him into the vehicle, into the passenger's side. 'We'll get the food and water,' said Tay. 'Uncle, you stay with him, while we fetch the supplies from the kitchen.'

It didn't cross her mind that she was talking to an animal.

'Wait,' muttered Clint. 'Wait, Tay. There's one thing—' He grabbed her arm, in a grip that must have hurt his hands, but he didn't notice. 'Go back up into the loft. Get up into the kitchen loft, *this is important*. There's a package, wrapped in black plastic. Papers. We have to take that with us. Important . . . What I saved is *very important*.'

Donny was scared and bewildered, but he wasn't going to break down. He and Tay hurried back to the kitchen house together, by silent consent taking a route that didn't lead them past the home bungalow. Tay wondered if they should have looked for more bodies. But she couldn't face that. Clint had said that everyone had been taken away.

She shut her mind to the meteor hole where the telecoms suite used to be.

Hostages. *Believe it.*

Tay went up into the loft and found Clint's package, while Donny finished packing the big rucksack and Tay's pack. (His own was useless, after having served as a fire-shoe.) They took it all to the garage. There were a couple of blankets in the old Land Rover that had been used when it was transporting baby apes around the clearing: they might come in useful. Donny and Uncle climbed in the back. Tay got behind the wheel, reaching for the pedals with her feet. She concentrated, bringing everything she'd learned – from Dad and from watching other people drive – to the forefront of her mind. She turned the key. The engine started at once. The gauge said the petrol tank was nearly full.

'I can do it,' she said.

'*Allah akbar!*' said Dr Suritobo, with something like a real smile, though his eyes were dark with pain and sorrow. God is great. Then he remembered his Clint voice. 'Move 'em on, head 'em out. Keep them dogies moving. Drive 'em, cowgirl.'

'*Raw*hide!' grinned Tay.

She drove out of the garage, crossing the concrete doorsill with a jolt, and headed for the open gates. It felt like being in charge of a huge dog that was pulling on its lead, but it was an obedient dog. At least, fairly obedient.

Please, don't let anything go wrong. Let us get to the research station safely.

They were heading into the wake of the fire. On either side of the track, charred and smouldering trees vanished into a fog of smoke and condensation. The sky was a pall of grey, with red-shot cloud churning through it. There had never been a fire this big near the Refuge, as long as they had lived here. Tay thought of satellite pictures she'd seen of burning rainforest, how small the jagged little patches of smoke and flame could look. Down on the ground, you couldn't see the edges. You couldn't know how far it went on, or how the wall of fire might twist and turn. Clint tried to raise a station on the old Land Rover's radio. He couldn't find anything but static. *A car will drive straight along a straight road*, Tay muttered under her breath, her knuckles white on the steering wheel. *Don't oversteer.* She could hear her father's voice in her mind: a warm voice, sometimes hasty, sometimes absentminded. Oh, my daddy . . . *Get used to the noise of the engine, change gear when it doesn't sound easy. Slow down into a bend, accelerate as you come out.* She was crying, she needed to wipe her eyes, but she didn't dare take her hands off the wheel, so she just had to let the tears fall.

Clint gave up on the radio. Tay couldn't talk because she was concentrating so hard. Clint didn't talk because (she was afraid) he was nearly fainting. His head kept dropping and then jerking back up, as he tried to stay conscious. She could only watch him out of the corner of her eye; there was nothing she could do to help. Donny and Uncle were so quiet in the back that she wondered if they'd gone to sleep. One kilometre, two kilometres, five kilometres. Six, seven. This is going to take ages, she thought, because I daren't speed up. But we'll keep on. Like this, steadily munching away at the distance. The kilometres will pass, and we'll get there—

After eight kilometres the Refuge track struck the back-country route that led in one direction towards Kandah City, and in the other direction to the north-east coast, where the Marine and Shore station was moored. There was a modern, main highway along the coast, but to reach it you had to go through the city. The back-country road was hardly different from the track, except it was wider. What if it was blocked by fire? Tay hesitated, wondering one last time if she should head for Kandah City. But Clint hardly seemed conscious, she couldn't ask him. She turned to the east. There wasn't another vehicle in sight. No sign of government soldiers, or of the rebels. No sound of planes or helicopters overhead. What'll we do if we catch up with the fire? What if the wind changes, and it comes back this way?

It was afternoon now, and very hot. On either side of the road shattered trunks lay among the blackened ranks of trees that hadn't fallen. In the blur of heat and smoky fog ahead she saw what she thought was one of these dreadful obstacles, right in their path.

Now what are we going to do?

Beside her, Clint roused himself with a deep sigh.

The fog had deceived her. It wasn't a fallen tree. It was another vehicle. Soon she could see the figures with rifles, waiting to flag them down.

'Tay, get into the back,' said Clint. 'Hide under those blankets.'

'I can talk to them. You're hurt.'

'Do as I tell you. And, if things go wrong, if I say run, you take Donny and Uncle and *you run for it*. You hear?'

'They can run. I *won't*. I can talk to them. I won't leave you.'

57

'Tay, you *must*. You are . . . you are so *precious*—'

'What? What do you mean?' She stared at him, words she'd vowed never to speak bursting out of her mouth. 'Because I'm a prize Lifeforce publicity stunt? I have to be saved because I'm one of the famous clones? Does that make me worth more than if I was a real human being?'

'Get in the back,' said Clint, in a tone that brooked no argument.

Tay scrambled into the back. Clint took hold of the steering wheel, and eased himself into the driver's seat. She crouched on the floor, under the animal-smelling blankets. The corner of Clint's package, which she had tucked into the waistband of her shorts, was digging into her ribs. She could hardly breathe. She'd been terrified while she was driving, but at least she'd been in control. The feeling of not being in control was unbearable.

They stopped. Tay heard one of the men with rifles talking to Clint. The man asked, quite politely, where Clint was going. Clint said he was heading for the river crossing that lay about thirty kilometres further along the road. He was asked where he'd come from, and he gave the name of a village back towards Kandah City. Then he was asked why he hadn't stayed at home. Didn't he know the People's Army had taken over this region, and there was a state of emergency? He said he hadn't known. They heard him switch the radio on and off. See, he said, my radio isn't working. I'm sorry. I'll turn back right now, I'll go straight home again—

The other voice, not so polite now, told him to get out of the Land Rover.

Clint argued, quietly, that he didn't want to get out of the Land Rover. He said it was an old Land Rover, and its brakes weren't too good, and also if he took his foot off the

58

gas, he wasn't sure if it would start again . . . But they made him get out.

Then the men with rifles saw how he was injured. Their voices changed a lot. Tay couldn't follow all that they were saying, but they were asking him again, *where do you come from?* They were saying he had a foreign accent. There was another voice, with more authority, asking Clint for his papers.

That's it, she thought. We're done for.

Clint's identity card would show that he was Indonesian, and these were the rebels who hated all foreigners. We *can't* run for it, she thought. We can't leave Clint, and anyway there's nowhere to run. But she got hold of the straps of her rucksack, which was on the floor between her and Donny, and started trying to open the offside door – Too late. The nearside back door was opened so sharply that Uncle and Donny almost fell out. There were yells of astonishment. Men with rifles grabbed at the ape, and the two children, and hauled them out on to the track.

'It's a man-of-the-forest!' they muttered to each other, in Malay . . . An *orang-utan*. 'It's from that crazy place! These are the English children from that orang-utan place!'

The men were slim and small, compared to Donny and Tay's dad and the other Europeans on the Refuge staff. They were dressed in camouflage, some of them had berets on their heads, but they didn't have any badges on their uniform. They didn't seem to know what to do with their new discovery. Tay's heart leapt in relief. They're not going to hurt us! But she was wrong, and her relief died at once. One of the rebels had twisted Clint's arm up behind his back; another man had Clint's papers, and that old-fashioned pistol. A third man, who seemed to be in charge, came over.

59

He gave the children and the ape a long, cold stare.

'So!' he said, in English. 'All *red monkeys* together.'

The others laughed. *Red monkey* was a rude Malay term for white people; and Uncle was a red ape. Very funny . . . Tay looked into their faces, and knew that these were some of the people who had attacked the Refuge. It was in their eyes. These were the rebels who had killed her mother and father, and Lucia Fernandez. They had killed innocent people, they had set the forest on fire, and they couldn't stop now. They had to go on, right or wrong . . . These thoughts ran through her head, with a strange *understanding* of how hard it is to stop once you've started doing terrible things, as she watched the officer (he seemed like an officer, though he had no badges of rank) reach to the shiny holster at his belt, and take out his gun.

The men around the children backed off, suddenly completely silent.

'You're the crazy ones,' said Clint, in Kandanese Malay, still polite but not grovelling. 'You don't want to harm these children. They have done nothing. Let them go.'

The man with no name doesn't ever say die.

But Tay saw the officer's eyes, and she knew what was going to happen.

He's going to shoot us. Right now.

Clint knew it too. He wrenched free from his captor, and leapt at the officer with the gun. 'Run, Tay!' he yelled, in English. '*Go*, kids!'

No one was touching the children. Tay snatched Donny's hand, and swung her rucksack at one soldier who tried to grab her, thumping him in the belly. The children went pounding across the grey, hot, ash-covered ground, ducking and diving between the charred trees. Yelling and gunfire came after them, but Tay kept going, clutching hold of Donny's hand, until the gunfire faded and a gulf opened under her feet. She thought she was falling. Instead she found herself stumbling down a steep, earthy bank, tumbling and stumbling, crashing through undergrowth, down and down, still clinging on to Donny's hand, into a deep gulley where the leaves were green, and the ground cool underfoot, and there was the sound of water.

They had landed on the bank of a stream. Thick vines and bushes closed off the slopes above them. There was no sign of the fire, except for a few charred twigs drifting on the clear, brown water. They listened for pursuit. Nothing happened.

'We can't leave Clint!' cried Donny. 'Why did you make us run away?'

'Because we were about to be killed,' said Tay. 'I'll go and see what happened.'

It was much harder climbing up the bank than coming down. Her arms and legs were trembling, and all her muscles felt weak. When she reached the top of the slope and peered through the trees she could see, through the murk, the old Refuge Land Rover, standing alone on the track.

'I need to have a closer look,' she whispered – as if Donny could still hear her. 'I've got to find out what happened to him.'

She crept up, sneaking from one burnt-out tree to the next. I can drive, she was thinking. We can still get out of here, and find help. When she was near enough to see that the rebels had shot out the tyres, she stopped. They'd shot holes in the petrol tank too. It hadn't caught fire, but it was leaking. There was a dark pool on the track. It reminded her of the pool of Clint's blood on the floor of the kitchen loft.

She could smell petrol, mingling with the ugly, incinerator stink of the burned-out forest.

The rebels' jeep was gone. There was no body on the ground.

They had taken Clint away.

She wiped her eyes. She hadn't realised that she was crying again.

When she got back to the bank of the stream, Donny was huddled up under one of the animal blankets. He must have been clutching it when they were dragged out of the Land Rover, and he hadn't let go. He had pulled it over his head, as if he was in bed, hiding from a nightmare; and he was shaking. She tugged it aside. Donny looked up and pushed the blanket away, embarrassed. 'Did they kill him?' he whispered. 'Did they shoot him?'

'There's no body. They just took him away. Like everyone from the Refuge.'

'Oh . . . Oh, that's good. At least he'll be with Mum and Dad.'

Tay put her arms round him. 'We're on our own, Donny. You and me. We'll have to look out for each other, and behave so Clint, and Mum, and Dad, and everyone, would be . . . will be proud of us, when this is all over. Do you agree to that?'

'Yes . . . I agree to that. Where's Uncle?'

'I don't know.' She hadn't noticed what had happened to Uncle. 'He's gone. He's a wild animal. I suppose he's doing whatever seems best to him. Remember what Clint said – the apes are free now. They have a chance, they might survive.'

Donny nodded. Tay started thinking over the contents of her rucksack. Matches, pocket-knife, compass, first aid kit. Some water and food. It was a pity they'd lost the bigger rucksack, with most of the supplies they'd collected in the kitchen. Was there a map? She hoped there was a map. Donny has a blanket. And we're *children*, she thought. We can avoid the rebels, and find ordinary people who will help us. We will make it . . . It was sad and peaceful in this hidden green valley. This is what Clint told me, she thought. The fire doesn't take everything. What survives will grow stronger.

'Tay,' said Donny, 'could you look at my back? I think something hit me when we were running. It doesn't hurt a lot, but it feels strange.'

She looked at his back. There was a red stain on his T-shirt. When she pulled it up she could see that he'd been hit by a bullet, under his left shoulderblade. The wound was small, and not bleeding much.

'You've been hit by a spent bullet,' she told him. 'I'll put antibiotic powder on it, and a dressing, and you'll be fine until we get to a hospital.'

'A spent bullet? That's what Clint had too. What does it mean, exactly?'

'A bullet at the end of its flight, with no strength left. It can't have hurt you much.'

She hoped she was right. She cleaned the wound, her second bullet wound of the day, and used the tweezers from the first aid kit to try and reach the bullet, if it was lodged inside. She couldn't find anything. Donny hardly whimpered. She didn't know if he was being incredibly brave, or if he was too shocked and exhausted to react.

They ate biscuits and drank some water, and rested through the heat of the day.

The afternoon grew cooler. Dusk began to fall, and Tay realised they were here for the night. No harm in that, she decided. They needed recovery time. She lay with her brother's head cuddled into her shoulder, and her arm around him. They talked about Clint, and how brave he had been. If he was still alive they would see him again, and he'd get a medal for bravery. They didn't talk about Mum and Dad, only about their friend Clint. That was all they could cope with for the moment.

At last they slept.

Three

Tay slept very lightly, and woke to the sound of birdcalls. She left Donny sleeping, found a place to get down to the water and washed her face and hands, cleaned her teeth with her finger, and took off her boots and socks to wash her feet. She felt much better after that. When she'd put her boots on again she looked in the rucksack, and thank God she'd not been imagining that she'd packed a map. A map of your area was basic survival kit, even though she and Donny had only been going to the caves. It was still there.

She spread it on the grass, and searched until she found a thin blue line flanked by tight contour lines, running roughly parallel to the back-country road to the coast. That had to be this stream, in its steep narrow valley – and they were in luck. The stream went on running parallel to the road, all the way until it ran down to join the Waruk, one of Kandah River Region's many rivers.

'What are you doing?' said Donny's voice. He was beside her, still wrapped in the grubby yellow blanket.

'Finding where we are. Look, it's going to be easy. We can stay off the road and follow this stream until it joins the big river, and we'll be at Aru Batur. You know, the river crossing, with the floating-bridge ferry. We might find people to help us there.'

Three summers ago, before Donny went to boarding school, the Marine and Shore station had been moored on the same coast. Pam Taylor had been there and the Walkers had gone to visit her, making an overland trek and camping out. It had been fun crossing the river at Aru Batur, on the giant raft they called their 'floating bridge'.

'What if we don't?' said Donny. 'What'll we do then?'

Aru Batur was the only settlement on the way to the coast, as far as Tay knew. She turned the map over. There was a smaller-scale map of the whole of Kandah on the other side, but it didn't tell her much. 'I'm not sure,' she admitted. 'We'll head for the river crossing. If we can't get help there, well, we'll carry on. We have a compass. It'll take us a few days, but we'll reach the Marine and Shore—'

'And then Pam will negotiate with the rebels, so Mum and Dad and everyone will be rescued? She can get Lifeforce to give them masses of money, can't she?'

'Yes,' said Tay, biting her lip, and trying to sound cheerful. 'That's what she'll do, right away.' She folded up the map: and then she jumped, startled. A shaggy, rust-red shape had suddenly appeared beside them, completely silently.

'Uncle!' cried Donny. 'Uncle! You came back! Oh, great!'

The ape sat with his long arms trailing as if they were broken. He looked at Tay, and made his Clint noise, in a questioning way, but without much hope.

Donny is a child, thought Tay. Uncle *knows*. She shook her head. 'I'm sorry,' she said.

It was hard not to believe that the ape understood her.

'They took him away,' explained Donny. 'The rebels kidnapped him.'

Uncle put his shaggy hands over his jowly face, looking so human in his grief it gave Tay a strange feeling. Then he raised his fingers to his mouth, several times, the way he'd done when he meant the ground was too hot to walk on. Ouch, ouch, ouch—

'Ouch, ouch, ouch,' said Tay. 'Me too, Uncle.'

Donny reached behind him. 'My back hurts,' he complained, but then he cheered up again. 'Hey, I just realised, now it doesn't matter that you don't know the way after the Waruk! Uncle will look after us. He'll be our trusty native guide.'

The ape was a wise and faithful friend, but he wouldn't make much of a guide. He'd hardly ever left the Refuge clearing. Tay was going to say this . . . but she changed her mind. She must not say negative things. They had to think positive. 'You're right. He'll be very useful. But now the native guide and the fugitives need some breakfast. Look in the pack, Donny, and choose something.'

'We can take turns to choose. It'll make eating more interesting.'

The three of them shared a tin of peaches and a packet of chocolate biscuits, and drank bottled water. They had water-purifying tablets, but they'd save them until their water bottles were empty.

'We'll try to walk fifteen kilometres today,' Tay said, as they packed up. 'We might not make that much, but it will be our goal, our personal best. That makes two days to the river. After the river crossing we can get back on the road, and we'll meet the Lifeforce people like Clint said. They'll be on their way to look for us.'

'Hey. You said we'd find help at Aru Batur.'

'I *didn't* say that, stupid! How could I know? I said I *hoped* we'd find help—'

The children looked at each other, and the beginnings of a squabble died. 'We mustn't get into arguments,' said Donny, very seriously.

'No. We mustn't. We'll stick it out, and be nice to each other, and behave so everyone would be proud, if we have to walk all the way to the Marine and Shore.'

'Let's shake on it,' said her brother.

They gripped hands, did the special Tay and Donny twist, broke the grip and knocked knuckles. 'We should do it with Uncle, too,' said Donny. 'He's part of the team.'

Uncle had gone to sit at the edge of the stream, but he was watching them.

He made his Clint noise again, very sadly.

For a moment, a picture of Dr 'Clint' Suritobo flashed into Tay's mind. His laughing face, his glossy black hair. How he'd been such fun to be with, always. And he was gone. It was all gone, everything . . . It hurt so much she was shocked. How could she keep going, with such pain inside? But she must.

'He mightn't want to do our handshake.' She didn't want Donny to be disappointed. 'He might think it's only for children, or only for humans.'

'Yes, he will do it. I'll teach him. It's the team sign. Come here, Uncle.'

The ape rose to his feet. Standing, he was about the same height as Donny, though broader across his shaggy chest and shoulders. He came up to the children, cocked his head, and made a face that was like the sad ghost of his old funny-lip. Then he gravely took Donny's hand, shook it, and did the Donny and Tay twist—

'Hey!' cried Donny, delighted. 'Look at that! He knows it already!'

'He must have watched us, lots of times,' said Tay.

But it seemed a good omen.

All three of them, in sequence, did the handshake, the twist, the rapped knuckles. The grip of Uncle's leathery hand was very strong. His wise and sorrowful eyes looked into hers. Uncle *knows*, she thought. He's hurting, just the way I am, and he may be an animal, but he's not a kid, he's a grown-up; and she felt stronger. Maybe it was stupid, but she felt she had someone she could depend on.

There was a pedometer on their compass, which Tay was wearing on her wrist. It let them keep track of their progress. They made good time through the morning. The grassy bank of the stream was as good as a smooth path, and it was a big improvement to be away from the smoke and ash. Tay carried the rucksack. Donny offered to take turns, but Tay thought he'd better not carry anything, because of the wound in his back. Donny wanted Uncle to take his turn, but Tay had visions of the ape vanishing into the forest with all their possessions. No matter how wise he was, he was still an animal, and he might decide to go off and survive on his own. She explained that orang-utans aren't built for carrying things on their backs.

Uncle wasn't built for walking, either, but that didn't matter. He took to the trees that closed off their gulley from the sky, and swung along overhead; sometimes completely silent, sometimes crashing through the branches as if he was making a noise deliberately, to cheer himself up. But every few minutes he would come plunging down again, landing on the grass and bouncing along beside the children for a few steps. 'To make sure we're okay,' said Donny. 'He's our babysitter, remember.'

The heat didn't bother them too much. The valley was shady and they were used to these temperatures. The pedometer counted the metres, and then the kilometres. Tay became obsessed with watching them mount up. When she noticed that Donny was lagging behind, she could hardly bear to stop, but she made herself be sensible and declared a lunch break. They sat on some roots and opened a tin of pears, while a butterfly with huge, lacy white wings drifted around them, as if curious to know what two children and an ape were doing here all alone.

Uncle refused the pears. Donny didn't finish his share. He said he wasn't hungry.

By mid-afternoon they'd covered ten kilometres, sometimes on smooth ground, sometimes clambering over roots and rocks, but always keeping close beside the stream. But Donny was tired. Tay was coaxing, nagging, praising and teasing him to keep him going. At twelve kilometres there was a change. The stream had grown to a small river, and the bank ahead was suddenly much rockier and steeper. Their path led over loose boulders, treacherously covered in big ferns and thorny creepers. Tay motored on, as fast as she could go without falling. She was worried about Uncle. She hoped he'd be able to feed himself, because they were going to run out of tinned food soon, at this rate. She was *very* worried about the river crossing. What if they got to Aru Batur, and it was in the hands of the rebels? How would they get across the river then? There were no bridges—

Then she realised Donny wasn't following her.

He was out of sight. She had to go back, and found him sitting on a rock before the boulders began, on a sandy beach in a curve of the stream.

'What's the matter? Why have you stopped? Come on!'

'Could we have a *short* rest?' asked Donny piteously.

'A little bit further.' Soon it would be dusk, and then they'd have to stop. But they wouldn't have done fifteen kilometres, and they *had* to do fifteen kilometres. 'Another thousand steps. We'll count them. They'll soon go. Then we'll have done thirteen kilometres. That's nearly as good as fifteen.'

When Donny was a little boy, and they were out on a trek in the forest, he'd get very tired. Dad used to sing nursery rhymes when he started to flag. Tay had never needed to be coaxed, no matter how hard or long the walk. She never ran out of energy.

'I'll sing "Ten Green Bottles"—'

Donny looked at her in despair; and then, as if he couldn't stop himself, he tumbled from his rock and lay on the ground, curled up in a ball. Uncle swung himself from the lowest branches of a tree and loped across the beach, knuckling the sand. He laid his long hand on the boy's shoulder and looked up at Tay reproachfully.

'I *know* he's tired,' said Tay. 'But we've got to get on. Get up, Donny, please.'

Donny didn't move. Tay heaved a sigh, and came down to the beach beside them. 'Please, please get up, Donny.' He didn't stir. She felt his forehead, and was shocked to find it was very hot, burning hot. He was shivering too—

'Oh no. He's got a fever. Oh, Donny, I'm sorry. I didn't know you were sick.'

She gave him aspirin and a drink of water, and coaxed him to suck two glucose tablets. When she rolled up his T-shirt to look at his back, only a tiny patch of blood had seeped through the dressing. She changed it anyway.

The wound looked no better and not much worse.

'Does it look bad?' Donny asked. 'It hurts. Sort of inside.'

'It doesn't look bad. Tell you what, we'll spend the night here. We've done well. Let me put some insect repellent on you.' Mosquito bites didn't usually bother the children. They had a regular vaccine injection that acted like repellent. But there was no point in taking chances. Feeling very guilty, she anointed Donny's exposed skin and made him the best bed she could, with the rucksack for a pillow and

71

the yellow blanket. She thought of making a fire, but they had seen enough of fire, and the night was warm enough . . . She told him how brave he'd been, and how they'd have a slower day tomorrow, and soon, soon they would be safe. He didn't seem interested. He curled up again, muttering that he couldn't get comfortable.

Tay went to sit on a boulder at the water's edge.

A new fear gripped her. *Donny's ill.*

Uncle appeared, silently, and hunkered down beside her.

'D'you think it's his hurt back?' she whispered. She knew she was talking to an animal: but she must talk to someone. 'Where the bullet hit him?'

The ape grunted softly, as if in answer.

'If there's a bullet, I can't reach it. It's buried too deep. What'll we do?'

Uncle said nothing. But his shaggy presence at her side was a great comfort. They sat together in silence until it was fully dark. Then Uncle went off into the trees, to sleep alone, the way orang-utans do. Tay lay beside Donny on the sand. In the middle of the night, she woke. Donny was sitting up, the blanket fallen back and his arms wrapped round his knees. 'Look!' he said. 'Look at the green star flowers! They're swimming across the night lake!'

The valley was very still and cool. In the clear darkness above the stream a ball of fireflies had gathered. There must have been a hundred of them, brilliant green like chips of emerald, spinning and whirling around each other, above their shimmering reflection.

'Isn't it beautiful!' said Donny. He grasped Tay's hand, smiling at her incredibly sweetly. His eyes, in the firefly light, were brimming with love and wonder. 'Twice. Here and there. Like in heaven. You see them, don't you Tay?'

'I can see them.'

'They're so beautiful. How unbelievably great to see that. Aren't we lucky!'

His skin was burning hot. She talked to him, but he kept telling her about the fireflies being stars on the night lake, no matter what she said. She thought he wasn't really awake. She wet her bandana in the stream, and bathed his face and hands. She did that again and again, with lots of fresh cool water, until he was quiet, and seemed to fall asleep again.

In the morning Donny said he was better, but the little wound on his back had gone puffy. Tay gave him more aspirin, and he ate a spoonful of rice pudding. Tay had no appetite. She finished the pears from the night before, but the pudding was like white slime. Uncle rejected it too, so they left the hardly touched tin behind, under a rock, and Tay felt very uneasy about the waste. What if they ran out of food? Then they'd have no energy for the trek at all. But if they could keep going, for just another fifteen kilometres, they'd reach the river crossing. She forgot that she'd been doubtful if anyone would help them at Aru Batur. Now it seemed like a haven that they *must reach*. There'd be people, there'd be some kind of medical help, a telephone that worked, maybe even a doctor . . . Donny didn't complain. He tried very hard to keep going. They walked slowly, and Tay sang to him, old baby songs, and he liked that.

Uncle stayed closer today. He was never out of sight.

By noon they'd covered five kilometres. They stopped for lunch, but Donny couldn't eat. Tay persuaded him to drink some water, and gave him two more aspirin. Then she left him with Uncle, and climbed up the side of the valley again. She was frightened of the rebels; but Donny needed medical attention. The climb was much further and steeper than it had been before, because they'd been travelling downhill all

73

the way, following the stream as it cut deeper and deeper into the valley. When she reached the top of the slope this time, she met an impenetrable wall of trees. They'd passed beyond the fire. It would be almost impossible to force a way back to the road.

Donny probably couldn't manage the climb, anyway.

They hadn't seen a human soul since they ran away from the rebels. Very few people lived in the forests of Eastern Kandah, except at the logging camps, and the villages at old river trading posts like Aru Batur. Tay stared at the trees, feeling the vast, lonely emptiness around her. The rainforest had been her home; now it felt like another enemy.

She went back to Donny, and told him they had to walk again.

By dusk they'd covered another three kilometres. Donny was being very brave, but she could tell that he was in pain. He said he couldn't get his breath. She coaxed him on, with her arm around him for the last part, until they reached another river-beach, where he would have a smooth place to lie down. She bathed his face and hands, wiped him with insect repellent, and made him as comfortable as she could. He drank some water, but he wouldn't suck any glucose tablets. He said he couldn't. He said his back was hurting, and his throat was hurting, and he couldn't get comfortable. Tay changed the dressing again. The wound had a swollen, angry patch around it.

Yet it looked so small, and it was only bleeding a very little.

Before they left the Refuge, Tay had put the first aid kit from the Land Rover into her rucksack. She'd used most of what was in her day-trip kit on Clint's leg wound. The Land Rover kit was much more serious. It was designed to cope with total emergencies, when someone was badly hurt and there was no chance of getting to a doctor. She left Donny, and carried the plastic box with her to the water's edge, where there was more light. She emptied it, looking for anything that might help. At the bottom of the box there was a flat case. She opened it, and looked at the contents. Morphine. A syringe and needles, in sterile packs. The powerful drug, in six small tubes. A leaflet of instructions.

Morphine is a very strong painkiller.

He would get a good night's sleep, she thought. I could give him morphine every night for six nights, and by then we'd have found a doctor.

A rust-red, shaggy, ape hand was suddenly there, beside her own. It looked like the hand of an ogre in a fairytale, beside her own small smooth human hand. Uncle deliberately picked up the syringe, in its packet.

'Hey. No! Put it down, Uncle. Put that down! Naughty!'

Uncle took no notice. He examined the wrapped syringe curiously, and then carefully replaced it in the case. He looked at Tay solemnly.

'You don't think so?' said Tay. 'You think I shouldn't give him the morphine?'

Uncle said nothing; he was only an animal. But he looked at her very severely. Tay shut the case and put it away, and took out the aspirin bottle instead.

'I think you're right. We'll save that for the last resort. I'll give him more aspirin.'

Uncle left them early that evening, and Tay missed him. She forced herself to eat a little, and got Donny to drink some glucose and water (she'd thought of dissolving the tablets in water, which was easier for him). She didn't sleep. She sat up all night, bathing his face and hands, and telling him stories, and reading to him from the copy of Shakespeare that she'd picked up in the clearing. The sound of her voice seemed to quiet him, although she didn't think he understood much of what she said. She managed to get him to drink more glucose and water, in the middle of the night.

If only there was a way she could give Donny some of her own strength.

But she couldn't.

In the early morning Uncle reappeared with a handful of bitter-smelling leaves. He gave some to Tay, and made her understand she was to chew them to a pulp, while he did the same, and then they would give Donny this chewed pulp.

Something had happened to Tay, when she and Uncle were looking at the morphine syringe together. This morning she could not think of him as an animal. An orang-utan isn't like a cat or a dog, or even a monkey . . . and Uncle wasn't like other orang-utans. He was like a person. A person like Tay, but older, and wiser, who would help her. She would take his advice—

Donny protested feebly about the disgusting green leaf-pulp.

Tay told him that orang-utans doctor themselves with herbs, and it would be all right, because the red apes were so like human beings, their medicine would be medicine for Donny. Uncle came from Sumatra, not from Borneo: but he and the other apes must have told each other things, secrets, wise things . . . She didn't know if she believed this reassurance herself. But she was desperate, and she truly didn't think Uncle's leaves would do any harm. Donny trusted her, and managed to swallow some of the goop. It had a good effect. His fever lessened, and he slept. But he obviously wasn't going to be walking anywhere today. Or the next day . . .

Tay thought hard, and made up her mind. They were

only ten kilometres from Aru Batur. But Donny might never get there at this rate.

She would trust Uncle to look after her brother. She would go and fetch help.

She told them what she'd decided. Donny said yes, he would like Tay to fetch a doctor, because his throat hurt. She wasn't sure he knew where he was. Maybe he thought he was at home, in the clearing, feeling poorly but safe in his bed.

Uncle didn't say anything, of course; but Tay was sure he understood.

The first two kilometres were lumpy going. Then she reached a tended patch of taro-root plants, and a footpath. She began to jog, and then to run, and the figures on the pedometer started flying. The heat of the day didn't slow her. She didn't feel it. She ran on and on. In another five kilometres the path became a wide track, and she reached a house: an old wooden house on stilts, standing in a garden of vegetables. There was no one in sight. She was frightened, thinking of rebel soldiers ready to jump out at her, but she was more frightened for Donny, so she went boldly into the garden, and up the steps, and called at the open door. Nobody answered. There were benches and a table in the room inside: coloured mats on the floor, enamel bowls on the table, a dish of rice, a clock on the wall. But nobody was home.

She hurried around the back: nobody there.

She ran on, speeding up. Almost immediately, she could smell smoke.

She passed more empty houses, and now she could see the smoke ahead of her, a cloud of it above the trees between her and the river. She had only been to Aru Batur once, on that overland trek to the coast, but she remembered it well.

There was a little mosque, and a blue-painted Christian chapel. It was unusual to have a mosque and a chapel in the same village, but Aru Batur was like that. It was a mixed settlement, a trading post. She remembered how they'd all eaten fried rice with great big fat river prawns at a market stall, on banana leaf plates, and Donny had played with the stallholder's children.

She kept running, through silent streets, past the mosque and the chapel, right down to the market on the waterfront.

All was still. The forest fire had not been through here, but another kind of fire was smouldering. There was a burned-out bus, oozing greasy smoke, standing in the market square. The stalls had been smashed, and there were heavy tracks everywhere, like the churned-up tracks in the Refuge clearing. She could see no human bodies, but there was a trail of dead chickens, and a dead goat. The beaten earth was strewn with vegetables, and fruit, and all kinds of market goods.

'Is there anybody here?' she called.

No answer.

'Help me!'

Her blood was drumming in her ears, the hot sun suddenly felt like a weight on her head. Everything she'd ever loved was falling away from her, falling into darkness, in this hot sun, in this stillness.

'Help me!' she yelled again. 'My brother's *dying*!'

No one answered. She heard a burst of gunfire, somewhere close. Undeterred, she hurried around, searching for some kind of help. There must be a pharmacy of some kind that she could loot for medicines. But she couldn't find it. The villagers had fled, everyone was gone, and she had to get back to Donny. She couldn't leave him alone with Uncle any longer.

Somehow, she'd have to get Donny here. They would find some medicines, she would break into one of the abandoned houses (Uncle would help, he was so strong), and they would put Donny to bed. If the rebels came back, too bad. It would be better to be kidnapped than to be on their own.

There was a rattling noise in the sky. She looked up and saw five big helicopters, sailing over her like giant vampire bats.

'Help!' yelled Tay recklessly, waving her arms. 'Help me!'

But they flew on, and disappeared towards the south.

She jogged all the way back to the river-beach, stopping only twice to drink some water. Donny was lying where she'd left him, with Uncle faithfully on guard. The ape had broken some green branches and woven them into a shelter, like the nests that orang-utans make to sleep in, high up in the trees, except this nest was on the ground. Donny seemed a little better, lying there in the cool shade with his blanket under him and folded over him. He must have been sleeping. He was glad to see her, but he didn't think she'd been gone very long. She told him she'd been to check out the river crossing, and it was safe, no rebels about; they would go there when he felt better.

She bathed his face and hands, and helped him up to have a wee. He said he wasn't hungry, but she gave him more aspirin, got him to drink glucose water, and even persuaded him to eat a piece from a new tin of fruit. The wound on his back was the same as it had been, only darker. She put some more antibiotic powder on it, and a fresh dressing. Donny winced, and whimpered, but didn't cry out.

Uncle and Tay stayed with him until he dozed off.

Then Tay looked at Uncle, grimly, and they went off to sit by the water.

'The rebels have been in Aru Batur,' said Tay, her head in her hands, staring at the calm stream. 'It was deserted. Either the people have all run away, or they've been kidnapped like everyone at the Refuge. What are we going to do? He's really sick, Uncle, and I can't get help. Have you got any ideas, because I don't know what to do.'

Uncle ducked his head, and made a very gloomy long-lip. She was sure he understood every word.

'I think he's got a bullet in his lung,' Tay blurted out, keeping her voice down so Donny couldn't hear. She'd been thinking this for a while, but she hadn't dared to say it, it was too awful. 'Maybe not a bullet in his lung, but something like that. Something that our first aid isn't helping at all. We can't move him, and there's no doctor we can fetch. But we have one chance, Uncle. The radiophone isn't any use. I've been trying and trying, in case, when Donny wasn't looking, but it's no good . . . But the phone has a GPS locator beacon, that means a little thing that's signalling our position all the time. I think it's still working. It's supposed to go on working for weeks. If anyone's *looking* for us, they can find us. We don't have to be on the east road.'

Uncle looked puzzled.

'Clint said Pam would move heaven and earth. He said we would go along the road and meet her, with Lifeforce people, coming to save us. We can't do that. We have to stay here, and look after Donny, and hope he gets better. But luckily someone might find us here, anyway. That's what I'm saying.'

She knew that Uncle agreed.

She forced herself to eat the rest of the tin of fruit. She wished she had the big rucksack, and it was full of sweets, instead of sensible things like baked beans, tinned pilchards and high-energy trekking bars. She thought she could have

80

persuaded Donny to eat a few sweets, and it would have been easier for her, too. But there was no big rucksack, and not much food at all that Donny could eat: a couple of sensible tins, biscuits, trekking bars and a good supply of glucose tablets. That was all.

At sunset Donny woke. She bathed his face and hands. He drank water and glucose but he sicked it up again. Tay had been refilling their waterbottles with purified river water, and it tasted horrible, but she couldn't help that. Uncle brought more of his medicine leaves. They managed to get Donny to swallow some chewed goop: but it had less effect than the first time. He had a high fever again, and he started crying. He'd developed a bad cough, which was making the pain worse. Tay propped him on a pillow made of sand and shored up with rocks, with the blanket wrapped around him, and told him stories, mostly about things that had happened when he was little. When she ran out of stories, she read to him from Shakespeare. He liked *A Midsummer Night's Dream*.

Donny was peaceful for an hour or so, but then he started crying again. 'I want to go to sleep, Tay, but it hurts! I'm sorry I'm being such a wuss, but I can't help it. I really can't. I didn't know anything could hurt this much. It's not *fair*.'

'Okay, you have to take some more of the leaf medicine.'

'It doesn't work. I won't eat it. It's for monkeys. It's all covered in monkey spit. Tay, you don't know how it hurts. It's horrible, horrible, horrible.'

There was a froth of bright blood at the corners of his mouth. She wiped it away with a tissue, and kissed his cheek. 'I'm just going to talk to Uncle for a moment.'

She went down to the beach, to the water's edge, taking the first aid kit with her. Behind her, Donny was crying; a sharp, miserable, hopeless sound, like an animal whining in a trap. The case with the morphine in it felt weirdly heavy when she took it out. She knew what was weighing it down. It was fear. Beside her, someone heaved a sigh. She was not startled. She was used to the silent way he would appear when she most needed him.

'What do you think?' whispered Tay. '*Should* I give him the morphine?'

She thought Uncle said yes. He was very wise, and he'd said no before: but now it was time. This was the last resort.

Tay gave Donny half of one of the ampoules of morphine. She knew how to do it. She was only fourteen, but her home was in the heart of a beautiful, remote wilderness. Mum and Dad had made sure that their children had emergency skills. And the children had been proud and happy together, sharing Mum and Dad's adventurous life.

When her brother was asleep she went to the river again, alone this time. The night was very still. Overhead there was a band of clear, dark blue sky. She could see a few stars. Dear God, she prayed. Please don't let this happen. But if it has to happen, please let me do it well. I want to do it well.

Tay and Uncle nursed Donny for three more days. On the first day Tay went to Aru Batur again. She found it as deserted as before, but now fires were smouldering in many of the abandoned houses. She didn't try to put them out. She left a message, written in English and Malay and held down by a stone, on a broken market stall, and she collected supplies. She didn't think this counted as stealing, and she wouldn't have cared anyway. On the way back she left a trail of markers; strips of cloth tied to trees and branches. Then she'd done everything she could think of, so she just stayed with Donny and gave him half an ampoule of morphine every six hours. She thought he had pneumonia now, but there were no drugs for that in the first aid. He never asked if he was dying, and Tay decided there was no reason to tell him. She told him he was too ill to move, and that she hoped help was coming. She didn't think he cared much. His world was reduced to being in pain, and fever dreams.

Uncle brought new green branches every morning, to shield Donny from the sun and rain. Towards the end, when Donny was very weak, the great ape sat for hours with the boy cuddled in his arms, holding him up so he could breathe. On the evening of the third day, Donny became quiet. He stopped crying, and he and Tay talked a little, about ordinary things. Funny things that had happened at his school, nice things they both remembered from Christmases, and birthdays, and holidays. He was lying propped up with his head on Tay's shoulder, and holding Uncle's hand, when he died.

The whole of that night, while she cried and cried, Tay planned to stay with her brother and guard his body, until the rebels came and found her or she died herself. But in the morning she knew she had to go on. She must tell someone what had happened. That was all she could do now for the people she loved. It was the only thing that made sense of being alive.

She thought they had to bury Donny. Uncle disagreed. He wanted to cover Donny in more green branches, as if he was sleeping. They argued about it, and at last they agreed to cover Donny in green branches, with the best presents they could spare him (the last tin of peaches, his torch, some flowers), and then bury the branches under a cairn of stones. Tay was dimly aware that she was making-believe that Uncle talked to her, and argued with her, but it didn't matter if she was pretending because it was *true* that Uncle cared. He didn't care like an animal, he cared like a person. The hardest part was when they had to cover Donny's face, and she knew that she would never, never see him again. But they did it, and they made the cairn. It took a long time, but they did it well.

Tay cried one last time, and then they set out together, the orang-utan with his immense strength, and Tay with her unquenchable energy, for the river crossing and whatever lay beyond.

They had to think of some way to cross the mighty Waruk river. The floating-bridge ferry that had carried vehicles at Aru Batur was grounded in the mud, tipped at a crazy angle. There were other rafts, motor boats and a few dug-out canoes, pulled up along the waterfront. Most of them, when you looked closely, had been put out of action in some way. Planks had been stoved in, fibreglass had been smashed, outboard motors had been wrecked. The river was wide, and the current was very strong. Tay paced up and down, while Uncle sat and watched from the boardwalk, his chin on his furry hands.

'One thing we mustn't do,' she told him. 'We mustn't lose the radiophone, because we mustn't lose the beacon. If we capsize, we can swim . . . but then we might lose the rucksack. Oh. Can you swim, Uncle?'

Uncle gestured reassuringly, *I'll be all right*.

'Now, if Pam was here . . .' She had thought she never wanted to see Pam Taylor again, or even think of her. But she could not bear to think of Donny, or Mum and Dad, or Clint, and she must think of someone. Everything she loved had been taken away, but she must keep cheerful, for Uncle's sake. She was the captain of this team. She had to keep up his morale.

'Pam would know what to do. You know, Uncle, she's

done some amazing things. Once she was on the coast of Vietnam, researching into the survival rate of the mangrove swamps, and she was stranded with a whole TV crew. Their support ship couldn't reach them, and tropical storms were lashing the coast, so she led the whole group through the swamps and over the mountains, and there were bandits and landmines, but she dealt with everything. There was a river that they had to cross, like this one, so she swam across it with a rope, and tied it to a tree on the other side, and then she made a harness to slide along the rope, so even the weakest TV person could be hauled across safely, and all the equipment too—'

When they'd been friends, Pam had used to tell Tay and Donny stories about her adventures as a conservation scientist. It had started when Tay was younger, so young she didn't know what was made-up and what was real. It had become very funny and silly, Pam giving herself the role of an action-movie hero, and inventing ever more wild, unlikely situations. Tay didn't know if she was making up a new story now, or if it was one she remembered. It didn't matter. It didn't matter if it was truth or fiction, so long as it made Uncle feel better. She wrapped her arms around herself, chilled by grief and helplessness. In the slick ooze under the waterfront boardwalk, little mudskippers hopped about. Donny used to love watching the muddy-mudskippers.

'You see, we're going to be all right because I'm a copy of Pam Taylor,' she explained, 'and she's a remarkable person. I'm an exact copy of a remarkable person. I hated it when I saw the "Teenage Clones Are Among Us" headlines. I felt as if my life had been taken away. But now my life *has* been taken away, no more stories, and it turns out it's a very good thing that I'm a photocopy of Pam. I don't have to wonder if I'm brave or clever. I know I am. So you don't have to worry. I can do this. I can get us through.'

Inside her, a voice was crying that she had not been able to save Donny's life. She had not been able to save Clint, or Lucia, or Mum, or Dad. But that was because she had not been remembering that she was really Pam Taylor. Taylor Walker was a helpless kid. Now the copy of Pam Taylor would take over, and she'd be able to do anything.

'That's why they called me Taylor, because I'm Pam's clone. I wished I had been called Mary after my mum, but I never told them that, because it would have upset everyone. I think they decided it was only fair to call me after her, because I was with Mum all the time, and they didn't want to call me Pam, because it would cause confusion. That's what I worked out. But I never asked. I don't like asking awkward questions. It might lead to talking about things . . . that . . . hurt.'

Uncle was watching her carefully.

'Don't look so worried, Uncle. I'm going to save us. I'm thinking.'

The metal ropes that had guided the ferry were still stretched across the huge, grey-brown face of the water. Tay selected a small raft, that didn't seem to have been damaged. She didn't trust the motorboats, and she didn't think she could handle one of the heavy dug-out canoes. She got Uncle to haul the raft along the mud to the waterline beside the ferry pier, and searched around until she found a length of rope. She slung her rope over one of the metal hawsers, brought both ends to the raft, and threaded one end between the bound poles that made the raft's raised side.

'Now we make a really good knot.' She was trying to knot the rope as she spoke – but she wasn't doing very well, because it was thick and hard, and her hands were small.

'We push our raft into the water, and we pole it across. I know how to do that. But we'll be fastened to the ferry-hawser all the time, like the harness Pam made in Vietnam. So we can't get swept away. You'll be quite safe. Do you see?'

Uncle looked closely at the really good knot, stuck his lip out, and started to undo it.

'Hey! Stop that!'

But he was tying the knot again, and doing it much better than Tay.

'Oh, I see. I'm sorry, thank you.'

The rucksack was on the boardwalk. Uncle had been carrying it. After Donny died, Tay had forgotten that orang-utans don't carry rucksacks. She'd been letting him take turns. He was part of the team, after all. She fetched it and put it on her own back, making sure the waistband was clipped tight. They shoved the raft out into the water – Uncle did most of the shoving – and scrambled on board. At once, caught by a powerful eddy, it began to swing around like a live thing. But it couldn't get free, and the looped rope slid along the hawser, just the way it was supposed to do.

'Aru Batur,' whispered Tay, staring passionately at the shore she was leaving. 'I'll come back, Donny. We'll come back for you, my little brother.'

Then the river took over, and she could think of nothing except trying to keep the raft steady, and keep the rope moving along. Uncle sat clinging to the side, staring at the rushing water with an expression of horror. Tay stood in the middle of the raft with her pole. The river was deep, deeper than Tay could guess, and the current was fierce. She fought doggedly, gritting her teeth and muttering *I'm a copy of a remarkable person!* But her arms got very tired; and this time Uncle couldn't help.

About two-thirds of the way across, they had a disaster. A massive tree trunk came racing towards them, from upstream. Tay thought it was going to swing by without touching them, but it had branches sticking out of it that were hidden under the surface. A snag caught them and dragged the raft sideways. Tay lost her footing and dropped the pole. It was lucky she did, or she'd have been left stranded, hanging on to it in mid-stream. The tree trunk snatched the raft away so violently that the guide-rope parted. The drowned tree and the raft went whirling around, all tangled together, Tay and Uncle being flung about like rag dolls—

'Push it off us! Push it off us!' yelled Tay. But the tree trunk, unbalanced by its new burden, heaved itself up, tipping the raft upside down. The water closed over Tay's head. She popped up to the surface and saw Uncle, caught in the branches of the drowned tree, staring at her, terrified, as he was swept away.

'I'm coming!' she yelled. 'Hang on!'

She struck out. She couldn't fight the current, so she had to let it take her, straight into the arms of the raft-snatcher tree. In a confusion of splashing, with brown foamy water in her throat and nose and eyes, she grabbed on to a branch and clung there.

'Jump!' she yelled. 'You've got to jump, Uncle! There's rapids and you'll get killed. Come on, remember I'm really Pam, I can save us, only JUMP!'

—and he was in the water with her, grabbing onto her frantically.

'Kick for the bank!' she screamed, and choked, and went under—

Somehow, between them, they managed it. They escaped from the current. They drifted, they swam, and at last they clambered out, into the waterlogged roots of the trees on the eastern bank, and up onto solid ground.

Tay crouched on her hands and knees, and threw up a lot of muddy water.

'Have I still got the rucksack?' she croaked. She was too dizzy to tell.

Uncle took her hand, and held it to the straps. Yes, she still had the rucksack. When she could manage to see straight, she took it off and checked to see what had survived. The radiophone was safe, and her torch, both still wrapped in plastic bags, but wet through anyway. Tins of food, a water bottle, the map and the piece of Donny's blanket that she had brought with her, to have something of his . . . The Shakespeare, very bedraggled. The compass was zipped into her shorts pocket, with her pocket knife and the matches. The map was useless. What was missing? She was sure there should be something else. Something important.

'Oh, Uncle! We've lost Clint's important papers! They were in here, I'm sure. Do you remember when you last saw them?'

She couldn't remember when she'd last seen that slick black package. She asked Uncle again, but he just offered her the Shakespeare.

'Not the book. *Different* papers with writing. Clint's papers—'

Uncle held out his empty hands.

'No, I don't remember either. Oh well, it doesn't matter. There's nothing to be done.'

Tay had looted the shops at Aru Batur. She didn't think that was wrong. She'd filled the rucksack with supplies again. Some of the stuff she'd looted was at the bottom of the river now, but they could still survive for days and days.

89

All she had to do was keep Uncle cheerful, and keep them both going. If they'd managed to stay attached to the ferry hawser, there'd have been a road in front of them now. But they'd been swept downstream, so instead there was another wall of trees.

'It's not as bad as it looks,' she told him, forgetting that to Uncle the trees were his natural home. 'There's only a thin band of forest here. Then it's the dry corner of Kandah. It's open country, savannah: low hills and a few trees but mostly grass. I don't think we should try to get back to the road now. We're better off just heading east by our compass. We'll come out of the trees soon, and then we'll be able to see for miles.'

Uncle took to the branches, Tay found the best route she could. The shy animals and birds of the forest floor didn't show themselves, but she heard them rustling and stirring, and that made her feel at home. Hornbills called, and once a troupe of monkeys crashed by, out of sight overhead. The going wasn't hard. There were paths, made by animals or people, and she just switched from one to another, keeping her heading near to the east. They had left Donny's grave at dawn. Before sunset, quite unexpectedly, Tay reached the eaves of the forest. She stood looking out over a wide-open country, under a sky coloured green and pink with the reflected sunset.

Uncle was suddenly beside her, appearing silently as he always did.

'Over there,' said Tay, pointing. 'That's where we're going. That's where the coast is. There's nothing to stop us now.'

She lay down, head buried in her arms, and began to cry.

The orang-utan crouched beside her, and patted her shoulder gently.

*

They rested overnight. At dawn Tay decided they should still follow the compass, rather than try to get back to the road. The ruined map was no use, but if they simply kept going east they must hit the coastal highway, and then they couldn't help finding the Marine and Shore station's mooring. She thought it was about a hundred kilometres. Say, five days walking . . . She explained this to Uncle, making it sound as easy as she could.

The savannah country of the 'dry corner' of Kandah was very hot in this season. Tay cut her piece of Donny's blanket in two, gave half to Uncle, and told him he should wrap it around his head and shoulders. He understood her very quickly. Then she walked, stubbornly, through the straw-coloured scrub, and the ape kept pace with her, until the heat was so great it was frightening. They took shelter under an acacia tree. The earth was red and cracked, it reminded Tay of burned flesh.

'We'll need to find water,' said Tay. 'We'll find some roots for you to eat. We'll dig for edible roots in the ground. Once, when Pam Taylor was—'

She couldn't remember the story. She took out the Shakespeare and read some of *Henry V* to him instead. Uncle listened attentively.

When she was tired of reading, she gave him the book. He turned the pages carefully, one by one, but he wouldn't read aloud—

She had been drinking water, but she hadn't eaten anything since before Donny died. She had no appetite, but she opened a tin and forced herself to eat so Uncle wouldn't be worried. The sun dazzled through the branches of the acacia. Tay felt as if she was falling apart, dissolving into the hot whiteness. She decided she'd better start walking again. She must keep on. That's all there was left. Everything else was gone.

'I knew there was something wrong with me,' she said. 'When I was a very little girl I knew, because of the blood samples and things. When Donny was a baby, I noticed *he* didn't have to have bits of him sent away to the labs: that's how I knew. I was afraid it meant I was going to die. Then they told me I was a test-tube baby, and I was sad, but I thought it was okay really. And then they told me I had no father, and I still thought it was okay, because it was a great achievement and a medical benefit, and I don't remember everything they said, but . . . Then I saw the headlines in the newspapers and I don't know why, but I suddenly felt so awful.'

She had tried to keep her fears to herself, because she knew that Mum and Dad loved her, and she didn't want them to feel bad. But now everything had been stripped away. She had nothing left but the truth.

'Maybe it's because I know I can't have a normal life. They say Lifeforce will protect me, but they've told everyone about the clones now, and of course people will find out who we are, me and the other four, and come after us, and make our lives a misery—'

The heat was so fierce that her sweat had dried up. She sat down, in the crackling grass, under the dazzling sun. She ought to get into the shade . . .

Uncle was there, watching her sadly.

'Do you know what a clone is?' she said. 'It's the artificial production of an embryo that is genetically identical to a pre-existing organism. But clones happen naturally all the time. Identical twins are clones of each other. Plants that grow from cuttings are clones. Human beings aren't clones, because human beings are supposed to be different from each other, and I'm not different from Pam. You know what that means? It means I'm not a human being.' She looked at her hands, and realised that under the brown, dirty skin there must be wires and little tubes. She imagined that in each of the tiny little tubes there would be a face. It would be the face she could see in a mirror, but it didn't belong to her.

'I wanted to ask them, *why did you do this to me?* But I can't ask them why, because there isn't any "me". I'm not a real person, I'm a thing.'

She dug in her pocket, pulled out her knife and opened it.

Uncle drew in his breath with a worried ssushhing noise.

'Don't be scared, I'm not doing any harm. I just want to see the wires.'

She held out her left hand, and sliced the knife blade down. She didn't feel any pain. She couldn't feel pain; she was only a clone. She couldn't see the wires, so she lifted the blade to slice again. She wasn't trying to hurt herself – she just wanted to see the truth. She was so absorbed in what she was doing, she yelled aloud when something suddenly grabbed her. It was Uncle. She struggled, crying and yelling, but Uncle was much stronger. He took the knife.

'Give it back!' she screamed.

The great ape bared his teeth at her. He threw the knife, so it flew away in a wide arc and vanished. He held Tay's right hand to his furry cheek, crooning at her gently.

Blood dripped from her cut palm. *Now* it was hurting.

'Oh *Donny*. Donny. Mum and Dad. Clint . . . You're all gone. I'll never see you again!'

Uncle put his arm around her, and raised her to her feet. She wept against his shoulder as he led her to a patch of shade. There they sat, huddled together, until dusk.

Then they walked, until it was very dark.

They rested until it started to get light: then they walked, until the sun was hot. Tay talked to Uncle, and Uncle talked to her. She knew he spoke. He told her that the two of them must not die, they must live and keep going, because otherwise nobody would know. Tay told him about sitting in the car park in Kandah City with Donny, the day Donny came home for the summer holidays. She had felt as if she was a package – with something *not human* inside. She was still a package, but now she was a package carrying all the people she loved.

Donny and Tay, and Dad, and Mum. And Clint, and Lucia, and everyone—

So many different memories, like different faces of a jewel. She held within her the last time she had seen Mum's face . . . The last time she had seen her dad, grinning and waving as he counted the votes for the Saturday night movie. She held within her Donny, and the way he had smiled the night when they had watched the fireflies. These memories were as good as DNA; they didn't belong to anybody else, they didn't belong to Pam Taylor. She remembered her dad saying *'it's not the DNA, it's what you do with it'*. This must be what he had meant. She would never have thought it all out herself, she was too tired and thirsty, but when Uncle had explained it to her, she understood.

She walked. When it was so dark that she couldn't see, she lay down and slept. When there was light, she ate something and walked again. Uncle was always beside her, and for his sake she had to keep going. She had to eat, and persuade him to eat. When their water bottle was getting empty, she wouldn't have cared. But she had to look after Uncle, so she had to search until they found a pool where she could fill it.

They had long, serious conversations.

Sometimes they saw wild buffalo; or a wild pig family

would charge out of the straw-dry grass and thunder away, curly tails in the air. Once there were helicopters in the sky; and then Tay and Uncle hid themselves. Maybe they walked two days, maybe for several days. Time didn't have much meaning in the journey Tay was making. The numbers on the pedometer made no sense: she wasn't sure how to tell which way was east on the compass any more. It didn't seem to matter.

The second waterhole was a churned and trampled mud patch in a dell among starved-looking trees, with a shrunken pool in the middle. Tay drank, and filled their bottle. Dimly, dimly, she remembered: the second waterhole is near the coast.

'We're nearly there,' she said to Uncle, as she sat on a boulder by the side of the pool, in the first light of dawn. She tried to smile for him, and her parched, sunburned face cracked like a dry leaf. 'You see, I told you. I'm a copy of a very remarkable person, and I have DNA memories all of my own, and you are a very remarkable orang-utan. We belong together, you and I. We're both of us *real people* now.'

She walked again, until her legs gave way under her, and then she slept where she fell.

When she woke up it was another day and she was completely alone. The water bottle was by her head. It was empty. The rucksack was beside her. She searched through it. There was no water, and no food except one battered trekking bar. Her mouth was cracked and sore, inside and out.

'Uncle!' she called. 'Uncle, where are you?'

Her voice came out as a faint croak. The rolling golden-burned grassland stretched away, empty to the horizon. The trekking bar had been soaked at the river crossing, and dried out again. When she opened the packet, straw-dry fragments crumbled on to her palm. She tried to lick them up but her tongue was too parched.

'Uncle!!!'

Uncle's gone to fetch help, she thought. When he didn't come back, she decided she'd better go and look for him. She had to lighten her pack; she was getting weak. She threw away everything except for the piece of Donny's blanket and the radiophone. The sun was beating down on her and it was hard to think clearly. She walked around in circles, holding the radiophone, and calling *hello, hello*. Nothing happened, and she'd forgotten about the GPS beacon. The phone felt very heavy, so she threw it away.

Soon I'm going to die, she thought. She didn't mind. She'd tried her best. She hoped Uncle had made it through. He would have to be the one to tell their story.

Then she was walking across some flat ground that seemed strangely cooler. There was a roaring in her ears, a haze in her vision, and the taste of salt on her scorched lips. She didn't see the dark shape of the Lifeforce Land Rover come shimmering out of the heat until it was nearly on top of her. People jumped out of it. 'Help me!' she croaked. 'Please help me! Everyone's been kidnapped. My mum and dad, and Donny and Uncle, and everyone. We have to find them.'

Suddenly the world was full of faces and they looked so strange – smooth-skinned, with no red hair, noses that stuck out, thin cheeks and small mouths, and such weird eyes.

'Where's Uncle?' she asked. 'Did you find Uncle?'

'Uncle is okay,' said a voice that was magically familiar. 'He found us. He's safe.'

Someone had picked Tay up, or she had fallen down: she wasn't sure which. A face that was like her own face grown-up, looked down at her. It broke into a photomosaic, hundreds of images, all the same face, all the same eyes, full of grief, looking at her with love and understanding. Tay began to cry, the sobs hurting her dry throat. Pam Taylor held her, in a hug that grew tighter and tighter. The babble of strange voices faded. Someone was dripping water into her mouth. She was a package, full of grief and loss, a terrible story that must be told, and after that a great blank—

But for this moment, she only knew that she was found.

Four

For two days (she found out afterwards it had been two days) Tay slept, and half-woke, and slept again. She had been bathed and put to bed, like a baby. She sipped broth, and drank milk. The scorched, baked skin of her face and lips, and hands and feet, was cleaned and soothed. She was told later that when they'd found her she'd been barefoot. They'd found her boots where they'd found her phone; but she couldn't remember taking the boots off, or why she'd done that. Sometimes she heard voices, and sometimes she even spoke to the people caring for her, but they didn't come into focus. She dreamed a lot when she was asleep, but when she was half-awake she couldn't remember the dreams: she could only feel them there, vague and cloudy in her mind.

At last she dreamed very clearly that she was standing with Uncle, on the eaves of the forest. Ahead of them was the lonely, golden country of the savannah. Behind them was their beloved home. Both of them knew that once they had stepped out of the trees they would never, never return. The clearing in the beautiful forest would be gone forever, because they would start to forget. The great majestic trees, stately guardians of life, the butterflies, the caves in the outcrop, the singing gibbons in the bamboo stand, the silence in the deep green shadows: everything would start to fade, if they took one more step. But they had to go on, because there was no way back, and if they didn't go on nothing new would be born.

We have to go on, Uncle, Tay murmured in her dream. We *choose* to go on.

Then she woke up. She was lying in a bed, under a clean white coverlet, and Pam Taylor was sitting in a chair beside her, holding her hand.

'Where's Uncle?' she said at once.

'He's safe,' said Pam. 'You won't remember, but I told you when we found you. It was Uncle who came to us. We've had to leave our mooring, because the army isn't in control of East Kandah. We're out at sea . . . Three days ago someone on deck saw an orang-utan, wandering on the shore. We couldn't believe our eyes: we came ashore and it was Uncle. Then we started looking for whoever might have brought him here. We thought of your phone, we traced the signal . . . and then we found you.'

'Uncle told you I was with him?'

Pam smiled, 'Well, he didn't exactly *tell* us—'

'Can I see him? Can he come and see me?'

'You can see him soon.'

There was something wrong. Tay could feel it. But she let the wrongness about Uncle go by, until she was stronger. She closed her eyes, then opened them again and looked around. The room was small, with greeny-white walls. There was one window. It was round and blue. Two shades, with a gently moving horizon between. Of course, she thought. I'm on a ship. I'm on the Marine and Shore. It seemed right to be at sea. Between her past, and her future. Between what had been, and whatever might be.

'Is there any news of . . . of my mum and dad, and Clint and everyone?'

'No,' said Pam. 'I'm sorry, no news yet. No bad news, no good news. The rebels are still in charge in Kandah River Region. No one can get near the Refuge, and we don't know where the kidnapped staff were taken.'

'We told you about Donny, didn't we?'

'Yes,' said Pam, squeezing her hand. 'Yes, you told us, darling.'

Donny is dead. My little brother is dead.

'Did you know the Refuge had been attacked?' she asked, after a silence. 'I expect you already told me, but I don't remember. Tell me again.'

'We knew,' said Pam. 'The first anyone outside knew of the attack was a call to Singapore. Mary and Ben had locked themselves in the telecoms suite. They were trying to save what they could of their work, and raise the alarm. They couldn't get through to me, or to Kandah City, but they managed to get through to Rei, in the Lifeforce headquarters building, in Singapore. They were talking to her when—'

Tay could bear to know what was probably, almost certainly true. She couldn't bear to hear Pam say, *there was an explosion*. Not now, not yet.

'They were cut off,' said Pam. Their eyes met, and they understood each other perfectly. 'Your mum and dad had said that the rebels were rounding up the staff, the apes had been released and that Lucia had been shot. Rei called us, and then the Sultan. But the Kandanese Army was fighting in Kandah City . . . and that was all we knew, for two days. Then we heard that the rebels had made contact, and the Refuge staff were being held hostage. Ben and Mary had told Rei that you two – you and Donny – weren't on site when the attack came, you were at the caves. But the rebels said that they were holding *everyone*, including the white children. We believed them . . . until someone saw an orang-utan on the shore, where no wild ape would ever be.'

'I expect they said they'd caught us to make you pay a bigger ransom. What about Clint? He saved our lives. Do you know where he is? Where did the rebels take him?'

'We don't know. We're trying to find out, now we know he was taken prisoner.'

Their eyes met, again with the same message. We know what's probably happened to Clint, but we can still hope—

'We'll have to be patient, Tay. I think the Sultan is really doing everything he can to help us, but the Refuge staff are not his only problem. The army is getting the situation under control again. But we are foreigners, and we've been told to leave, to get away from Kandah's coastal waters, because they can't guarantee our safety—'

'But we'll stay!'

'Oh yes,' said Pam, grimly. 'We'll stay. If we'd left for Singapore when they told us, we wouldn't have been here to find *you*. I am going to keep the Marine and Shore as near to the coast as I dare, until I *know*. Ben and Mary thought that if we left we might never be allowed back, and I let them stay. Lifeforce is going to maintain a presence here, until I know what's happened to them and all their staff.'

Tay felt all the self-blame that Pam Taylor couldn't put into words, because then she would cry; and she mustn't cry. 'You didn't know the People's Army would attack an orang-utan Refuge. You couldn't have known that. It was crazy.'

'I should have known it was time to get everyone out. The alarm bells were ringing. I ignored them.' Pam shook her head. 'But that's my problem, Tay, not yours.'

'Is there a record of my mum and dad talking to Rei?'

'Yes, we do have a recording,' said Pam, gently. 'Of part

of it, anyway. You'll hear it, one day; and you'll be proud.
But not right now.'

'No,' agreed Tay. She knew she couldn't take it yet. 'Not
right now.' She swallowed back the tears and lay quietly,
thinking about the day that Donny had come home from
school, and all the bruised and bitter thoughts she'd had.
They were gone. She looked at the hand that was holding
hers. Bone of my bone, flesh of my flesh, she thought. All
her life there'd been this grown-up person *Pam*, who was
such a true friend, who seemed to know exactly how
things felt, who was like a mirror . . . Now she knew
why. She *understood*, which is different from knowing the
facts.

'When the story broke,' she said. 'I mean, the "teenage
clones" story, I was very angry. I couldn't help it. I thought I
never wanted to see you again.'

'Every one of you has reacted differently,' said Pam. 'All
along. You're the one who has surprised us most, Tay. You
were always so cool and calm. But I knew how you must be
feeling, inside. I knew it would bust out sometime, and I
didn't blame you—'

'I don't want to hear about the others. That'll make me
feel weird again.'

'Tay, I'm sorry you have to be with me, if it makes things
harder—'

'No,' said Tay. 'I don't feel like that any more. When I
was on the trek, alone with Uncle, after Donny died, it all
came out. How . . . I thought I wasn't a real person, because
real people are different from each other, and I'm only a
copy. But DNA isn't what makes you a person. It's what
you do. Dad said that. I have memories that are all my own,
not yours. They're the blueprint of being me, same as DNA
is the blueprint that tells the cells how to develop.'

Pam was looking impressed. 'That's very good. A good way to think about it—'

'Yes.' She grinned, slightly. 'I didn't make it up myself. Uncle explained it to me.'

'Uncle?'

'Yeah. He was wonderful. I thought I was saving him . . . Now I know, of course, he was saving me. He let me help him, because he knew it helped me. He's *so wise*. We had such long conversations . . . and we read Shakespeare . . . and . . .'

Tay's words trailed away. Pam nodded, smiling very kindly. There was something Tay wanted to ask, only she hardly liked to say it. She hesitated. 'Would you mind . . . if I called you my mum? In m-my thoughts, I mean, not out loud. I know it would be stupid if I said it out loud. But j-just for a while?'

'You can call me Mum for as long as you like,' said Pam, the words bursting out of her, as if she'd been holding them back by force until this moment. 'I knew I couldn't have a big place in your life, Tay. I knew you belonged to Mary and Ben. But in my heart, I've called you my daughter since the day you were born. Since I saw you being born. Oh, Tay—'

Tay held out her arms. They hugged, with relief and joy, in the midst of all the tragedy. 'I'll *never* take Mary's place,' said Pam fiercely, her cheek pressed against Tay's hair. 'Never, never. Mary and Ben will *always be* your mum and dad—'

'I belong to them. And Donny. But you and me, we'll always have each other.'

'We'll always have each other.'

They let go, both of them embarrassed by this outburst, but very glad. Tay lay back, and Pam tucked the covers around her. 'Now I'm going to leave you for a while. I want

103

you to doze there and do nothing – except you can use the bathroom, which is through that door, and here's a pager: press a button if you need anything, and someone will come. I'll be back with some soup at lunchtime. If you're good, you can sit up and read in the afternoon, or I'll bring in a video-tv and you can watch a movie—'

'Not more soup.'

'Yes, more soup. It's the kind of food you need, after a trek like that.'

Pam stood up. Tay felt so many unanswered questions buzzing in her brain. Questions that must be answered before she could go on into that unknown country, beyond the eaves of the forest. Why did you let other people bring me up, if you loved me? Why did Lifeforce make me? Was it truly for the benefit of humankind, or just to see if they could? What kind of life am I going to have? Not yet. Not until she knew what had happened to Mum and Dad, and Clint.

But there were other things, less important things, that puzzled her.

'Are you sure I can see Uncle? Are you *sure* he's here and he's okay?'

'Of course I'm sure,' said Pam. 'He's very sad, poor old boy, but he's in safe keeping. You can see him soon.'

'All right.' Sleep was rushing over her again. 'Pam? How did anyone know?'

'How did we know what?'

'That I was with him?' said Tay. 'He *must* have told you. If he didn't tell you, how did you know to look for my beacon signal? You thought Donny and I were with the hostages.'

'Oh,' said Pam, looking slightly uneasy. 'I suppose that was me. Sometimes I, well . . . it seems as if I know things, if it's about you.' She left the room quickly.

Tay looked at the buttons on her pager, and the narrow door that must lead to the bathroom. She thought of her bedroom in the clearing, and all her possessions. Gone, all gone . . . She closed her eyes and drifted into sleep, her grief for Mum and Dad and Donny like a quiet, dark ocean that surrounded her, but would not drown her. But even in sleep a nagging worry about Uncle was troubling her, at the back of her mind.

Next day Tay was pronounced well enough to get up in the afternoon. She dressed in clothes that belonged to one of the Marine and Share lab assistants, who was slim and small enough to be the same size as Tay. It was great to be clean. She'd almost forgotten how it felt. She went in search of Pam Taylor; barefoot, because her European feet were too big for the lab assistant's sandals and too sore for boots.

The Marine and Shore station was a big ship. The helicopter pad, and the seawater tanks, were just part of the scenery on the forward section of the main deck. There were two decks of labs, besides the cabins, the bigger saloons, and the storage holds. Tay stood at the rail for a while, in the shade of one of the ship's boats, which were held up in the air over the deck, in the fat claws of the davits that would swing them down and launch them on the sea. She could hear Donny's voice. She could remember running around these fascinating cluttered decks with him . . . She stared at the golden shore of Kandah, across the calm, blue sea; and some part of her wished she was back there, alone with Uncle. Being lost means you only have to put one foot in front of the other. Being found means you have to deal with *everything*.

Marine and Shore people passed her, the crew and the science staff. They stopped and said admiring things about her trek, and that they were very sorry. Tay thanked them, because it seemed as if she had to thank them. Eventually she found Pam in one of the labs, alone and working at a microscope. Beside her, on the long counter, there was a row of small tanks, for live specimens. Tay looked into them. There were starfish, lurking in holes in pieces of coral rock, from which they reached out spidery crinkly-tentacled arms that were green or gold or red. They looked like wriggling bunches of underwater Christmas tinsel.

'You're still working on the brittle stars?' She knew about Pam's research.

'Mm,' said Pam. 'They're boring as pets, but they're a good indicator of the health of a tropic shoreline – and they have some interesting genes.'

'They're pretty.'

Pam switched off the microscope and pushed her chair back. She was wearing a lab coat today, over shorts and a T-shirt. She smiled, and Tay felt a jolt. *That's my smile.* Before she knew the complete truth, she'd known that she looked very like Pam. It hadn't bothered her; it had seemed natural. Now it seemed so weird.

She looked out of the window, trying to put the photocopy idea out of her mind.

The glass in the lab windows was solar-collecting, and polarised to shut out the glare. The burnt-gold shore was toned down to a muddy yellow, the sea looked dull.

'What's happened about the little girl who was born a medical clone in England?' she asked. 'I haven't seen any world news for ages. Is she all right?'

Another medical corporation had announced their first human clone-baby this year. This baby had an older sister, who was six years old and had a rare and terrible disease. If the older sister was to stay alive, she needed a transplant that only a genetically-identical twin could give her. That's why the parents had wanted a clone. The baby had been grown from one of her sister's cumulus cells, a special kind of cell best suited for the cloning treatment. The first ever human clone in the world . . . or so the makers had thought.

'She's doing well,' said Pam. 'She's a normal, healthy baby.'

Cloned animals sometimes have hidden defects that only appear when they are a few years old. That was one reason why people had said there should never be human clones. But there were better tests now, and better ways to start the embryo's development. The other medical corporation was certain that their baby would not have any problems.

'Is that why Lifeforce had to announce that we existed?' asked Tay. 'Because the other company had got in ahead of you?'

'Not exactly,' said Pam. 'We'd decided you should be anonymous, until you were old enough to deal with the flak. We succeeded, although of course there were rumours, but it's been getting difficult. When the Welcare Foundation broke *their* silence that was good, because it meant we could tell the world, and you five wouldn't have to bear the full weight of being the first.'

'So now a cloned baby really is just a special kind of test-tube baby.'

'That's how we'd felt all along.'

Tay went on staring out of the window. It isn't the same, she thought. It's not the same thing because it *feels* different. It feels different to *me*, standing here, to know I'm physically the same person as Pam. And I know it feels different to her, too.

'Do you think the parents of the Welcare baby were right to have her?' asked Pam, quietly. The baby didn't have a name in the news reports. She was 'The Welcare Baby'. Her real name was being protected. That was the way people were talking about Tay, too, all over the world. She was one of 'The Lifeforce Teenagers'.

'No. When she's older, she is going to know that no one wanted her for her own sake. She was made for her sister's sake. She's going to know that, all her life.'

'People have children for all kinds of reasons, Tay. Sometimes they have children without wanting them at all. That doesn't mean—'

Tay turned from the window and stared at the brittle stars. They didn't know that they were specimens in a lab. They thought they were normal animals, living for their own, starfish reasons, in a rock pool somewhere. She shouldn't have started talking about the Welcare Baby. She wanted to deal with everything, but she wasn't strong enough yet. Now she was choked up again, and *she didn't want to cry.*

'Let's go and see Uncle,' said Pam. 'I'll take you along to see Phillipe, to pay your respects, and then we can go and visit him.'

At the Refuge, things had been easy-going. Mum and Dad were in charge, there was no question about that, but everybody lived in the same conditions, everyone socialised together (the ones who wanted to be social) and pitched in, if necessary, on any kind of jobs. 'High-powered' people like Pam Taylor and Rei van der Hoort behaved like anyone else when they came visiting. At the Marine and Shore things were different. Dr Phillipe Levier was the director. He was strict and stiff; he ran things the way he liked them; and though Pam outranked him, he was in charge here. They went along to his office. Dr Levier said that he was very, very sorry, and he made a kind of speech about how much he had admired Tay's mum and dad. He kept on for about five minutes: it felt like hours. Tay just tried to think about something else. 'I'm sorry about that,' said Pam, under her breath, as she left the director's office.

'It's all right, I know people have to say those things.'

They went along a passage on the same level as Tay's cabin, but on the shore side of the ship. Pam knocked on a door. 'He's in a cabin because we don't have anywhere better,' she explained. 'The Marine and Shore station doesn't do captive studies of large mammals, and if they did, we couldn't put an orang-utan in the same accommodation you'd use for a dolphin—'

'Captive study?' said Tay. 'But Uncle's not a captive—'

The door was opened by one of the lab technicians.

'Hello Chen,' said Pam. 'This is Tay, our other brave survivor. How's the patient?'

Chen shook Tay's hand. 'What a hero. I'm so very sorry. The uncertainty must be terrible. Maybe you don't recall, but I was here the summer your family came. I met you and your brother. Very nice boy. All this, everything that's happened, very terrible.'

Tay was trying to look over his shoulder. She'd half-expected Uncle to open the cabin door, but he was nowhere to be seen. The cabin was like her own, except that there was a workstation desk, with a computer on it and some books, tucked beside the bunk.

'Tay,' said Pam, 'I ought to warn you, Uncle's not in very good spirits—'

There was an inner door leading to an adjoining cabin. It was standing open. The other room had been stripped bare. There was no mattress on the bunk: no chair, no workstation, no carpeting. Heaps of dry grass covered the floor, and a pile of tired-looking green branches lay on the bed. There was a bowl of fruit, an enamel bowl of water and a tin

109

mug. In one corner someone had strung up a piece of cargo net and a couple of knotted ropes.

Uncle was sitting on the bunk, beside the branches but not touching them. His chin was on his chest, his long arms lying slack, as if they were broken. He didn't look up.

Something inside Tay turned over. She felt suddenly, completely bewildered.

'Hello, Uncle?' said Chen, brightly. 'You've got visitors. Look, here's Tay!'

Tay couldn't speak. Uncle was . . . Uncle was . . .

'Uncle?' she managed to say, at last. 'Hello? It's me. It's Tay—'

The ape raised his head. His eyes moved listlessly, his glance passing over the three humans without a sign that he recognised any of them. He lifted his chin and scratched underneath it. Tay saw with a shock that there was a collar round his neck.

'We freshen the branches for him every day,' said Chen. 'And the bedding, of course. We've been taking the dinghy into shore, after dark, and making a quick trip to the nearest trees. We're not afraid of the rebels, but we don't want to be spotted by the Kandanese army helicopters—'

'They already think we're too near the coast,' said Pam.

'But he doesn't touch them,' said Chen, sadly. 'They're supposed to make nests out of branches, aren't they? I've, er, tried giving him toys as well. I know apes like toys.'

Tay noticed that there was a child's beach ball on the floor by the bunk, and a skipping rope, and a brightly-coloured plastic truck. The plastic truck made her especially mad. *Uncle is a grown-up! He's as old and wise as anyone—*

'Why is he like this?' she cried, the words coming out far too loud. 'Why are you keeping him locked up? *What have you done to him?*'

110

Uncle sat like a stone. Chen looked puzzled.

'We haven't done anything to him,' said Pam. 'Just done our best to make him comfortable. We tried having him on deck, but he's calmer down here. I'm sorry. I should have given you more warning, but I hoped he'd be different with you.'

'I know he was the Refuge mascot,' put in Chen. 'And very tame. Everyone knows about Uncle . . . but we can't seem to cheer him up, the poor old guy.'

'Uncle?' cried Tay. 'Oh, *Uncle*—'

She'd been standing in the doorway. She'd almost felt that she wasn't allowed to go into his cage (because the cabin seemed like a cage). She and Donny had never been allowed to go into the orphan apes' 'clubhouse'. She broke free from her shock, went to him and took his hand. It was too late. The ape's furred, leather-palmed hand lay dead in her grip. He wouldn't look at her. She should have run to him at once. Now he counted her the same as the other humans, who had put a collar on him and locked him up.

'You can't treat him like this! He isn't a wild animal! He won't attack anyone!'

Chen the technician and Pam Taylor looked at each other.

'Maybe we'd better leave him for the moment, Tay?' suggested Pam. 'He doesn't seem to be responding. You can come back another time.'

Tay heard the uneasiness under Pam's calm tone. An adult orang-utan is *extremely* strong, and Uncle did not seem to recognise the human girl as his friend. A shudder went through her. How could she be afraid of Uncle? But she was. She was afraid, because he was so different. She let go of his limp hand, but stayed, defiantly, crouched by the bunk.

111

'Uncle? *Please*? Look at me. We made it, Uncle. You saved us both—'

There was a patch of blue, half-hidden in the dry grass. She looked again, and saw it was her charred, battered pocket Shakespeare, with the blue cover. But how—? She'd thrown this book away. She *knew* she'd thrown it away, to lighten her pack.

'Uncle, where did you find the Shakespeare?'

'Oh, his book!' Chen exclaimed. 'That's his best toy. I don't know where it came from. One of his other keepers must have given it to him. We have a rota . . . He likes that book. I've seen him handling it.'

'It's mine. This is mine. We saved it from the Refuge.'

A flood of bitter, sweet memories came rushing into her mind. *Oh, the night when Donny died in our arms* . . . But if Uncle had the Shakespeare, then Uncle was . . . Uncle was . . . Was he *acting dumb*? But why? Why would he be doing that?

'Oh,' said Chen. 'Well, then I don't know how it got here. Please, take it.'

Suddenly the ape moved. He swung down from the bunk, scrambled over to his food bowl and sat like a russet-furred sack of potatoes, turning over the pieces of fruit.

'That's a *good* sign,' said Pam, with rather forced cheerfulness. 'He's eating. I really think we should leave him, Tay. You can come again tomorrow.'

Tay stood up and went back to the doorway, brushing dry grass from her knees. This felt so wrong and strange, she wondered if she was awake or dreaming. As she looked behind her she saw only an animal, a large ape sitting dull-eyed in his captivity, as if he'd never known anything else.

*

She told Pam she wanted to be alone, and fled to her own cabin.

The face in the mirror in her tiny closet of a bathroom was suntanned and sunburnt, with parched hair and hollow eyes, and a mouth fastened tight so that no tears or sobs could escape. She stared at herself, and for once – since she'd been told the truth – she wasn't thinking *my own face doesn't belong to me*. She was thinking of Uncle. An orang-utan face isn't pretty to human eyes. The nose is dinted in when it should jut out, the domed forehead looks clownish. The skin is slack and wrinkled, the male ape's cheekjowls look like unnatural growths. Tay was used to the apes, and saw them as individuals. After days alone with Uncle, she'd looked at human beings and seen *them* as comical and strange—

But seeing an ape as an individual isn't the same as—

Isn't the same as knowing that an ape is as intelligent as a human, despite his appearance.

'What's going on?' she whispered, aloud. 'What on earth's going on?'

She was still holding the pocket Shakespeare. It was falling apart, soaked by river water, dried by the sun. The pages were coming out in handfuls. She opened it, thinking of those long hours on the savannah, waiting for the sun to go down. Tay had read to Uncle, and then she'd given him the book. She remembered how he'd turned the pages, studying the washed-out print with such care. And here were his fingerprints, big rusty fingerprints, stained by the red earth . . .

I had *conversations* with him, she thought. Was I delirious, that whole time?

Someone tapped on her door.

'Come in.'

'Hi,' said Pam, shutting the door behind her. 'Are you okay? I wanted to say, I'm sorry about Uncle. I should have told you . . . but I didn't want to upset you. You said Uncle saved both of you, and I know it's true. I *know* how important he was to you. If there was anything more I could do, I'd do it. But I'm not an animal psychologist—'

'He doesn't need a psychologist. He needs to be treated like a person.'

Pam nodded. 'I know what you mean. He's imprinted on humans. That's why we have him in that double cabin, so there can be someone next door all the time. But he can't have the freedom he had at the Refuge. I'm sorry, but I can't do that. I'm not in charge here, you know. I don't know if it would make a difference, anyway. Animals can mourn, Tay, like human beings. I think he loved Clint, very deeply. They'd been together for years. Uncle is just very, very sad.'

Tay thought of the crossing of the Waruk river. How Uncle had tied the knots, how totally human he'd been in his terror of the water. She thought about the worst time of all, in the savannah, when she had really been falling apart. Uncle had taken the knife from her when she was cutting herself open to see the wires. She had cried on his shoulder!

'You don't understand,' she blurted out. 'There's something weird . . . At the Refuge I didn't know, I thought he was just very tame. On the trek he couldn't hide what he is; he had to let me find out. I told you how he was our guide, and how he looked after us. It was more than that, more than a faithful dog or something. I don't understand what's going on, but you have to believe me. *Uncle isn't an ordinary orang-utan.*'

'I know he's not ordinary. He's a hero—'

'No, you have to listen. He knows things. He came after us when we went to the caves, because he knew something

114

terrible was going to happen. He understands when you talk to him. He brought medicine leaves when Donny was ill, and showed me what to do, and he stopped me giving Donny the morphine until it was the last resort. He helped me bury my brother! He *talked* to me! He explained being a clone to me—!'

'Tay, calm down—'

Tay shook her head impatiently. 'Oh, I don't mean he spoke English! I know he can't do that. He doesn't have the right kind of mouth, or anything. It isn't sign language either, it isn't something he's been *trained* to do. He didn't talk out loud, but he talked and I understood. He didn't read aloud, either, but I saw him turning over the pages. It's because he's intelligent. I don't know how it happened, but he's intelligent like a person!'

'Tay,' said Pam. She took Tay's hand, led her to the bunk and sat down with her. 'What are you saying? You are not making sense, my dear.'

Tay had a sinking feeling: she knew she had started this all wrong.

'I know how it sounds, but I'm *not* making this up. I've lived with orang-utans half my life. I know what they can do, and what they can't do.' She drew a breath, and spoke very carefully and reasonably. 'On the journey here, with me, Uncle was more than a smart ape. He did things that no animal would do. I don't know how to explain it, but that's the truth. And *it's just horrible* for anyone to treat him like an animal. It must make him feel terrible. *That's* why he's the way he is!'

She was gripping Pam's hand too fiercely. She let go, and tried hard to look calm.

'I don't know what to say,' said Pam. 'Except, you can see him again tomorrow. We'll take him out on deck. He'll

115

have to be on a collar and lead . . . but maybe that will help.'

'You aren't listening!'

'I am. I'm hearing that you are very tired, and full of shock and grief. You've been through a tremendous physical and mental ordeal that would have floored anyone but you, and so has Uncle. You are still exhausted, and you're not thinking clearly. I hate to see Uncle suffering. I hope we can help him. I hope he can forget his sorrows, and have a long, happy life. But now I want you to lie down, and let me give you a mild sedative.'

Tay didn't protest. She felt terribly confused.

Days passed, and still there was no clear news about the Refuge staff. The Kandanese government was winning. The rebels were in retreat, and they were talking to Red Cross officials about the hostages, but they would only say that the Refuge staff were safe. They wouldn't give a list of names, and they wouldn't say where the prisoners were being held. The weather stayed calm and hot and dry; a stillness that seemed to mock the terrible anxiety of this waiting. Tay did not let herself cry. She was determined not to break down. She just wished she could stop herself from hoping that Mum and Dad were still alive.

When she'd been on the Marine and Shore for a week, Pam came to find her one morning, in the station's library. Tay was helping out the librarian, by doing some online filing. Everyone was trying to keep busy, though most of the station's research work was at a standstill. The librarian, after a brief word from Pam, went away and left them alone.

'Hi,' said Pam, sitting down. 'Tay, I want to talk to you.'

Tay had been back to see Uncle several times. She'd even been out with him once, when Chen took him round the deck on a collar and lead. She wouldn't do that again, it had felt totally horrible. She'd tried talking to him, she'd tried sitting with him in his cabin, silent like another ape. There was no change; nothing worked.

Nothing worked because she was never alone with him. The humans wouldn't let her be alone with him . . . And she could understand how the rest of the crew and the staff reacted. She could see that the idea of an ape being human must sound crazy. But she couldn't forgive Pam. Bone of my bone, flesh of my flesh, she thought, staring at her gene-mother. You *know* I'm telling the truth. How can you behave like this?

Tay needed desperately for someone to believe her. All she got was soothing words, and Pam basically saying she was having delusions.

'All right,' she said. 'Let's talk about Uncle. He thinks I've betrayed him.'

'Maybe we've all betrayed him,' muttered Pam, almost to herself. She sighed, and rubbed a hand behind her neck, rumpling her golden-brown hair. Tay didn't want to notice, but she couldn't help seeing the shadows under Pam's eyes, and the tightness around her mouth. That's how my face looks, she thought. When I'm trying not to cry.

'Tay, this isn't about Uncle. I have to . . . How much do you know about the way you came to be born? I have to ask you, because we've never talked about it—'

'It was in the 1980s,' said Tay, flatly. 'Lifeforce was trying to develop a gene-therapy cure for some disease or other. Volunteers from the company took a new drug, called M-389, and they got an incredibly good result. But it didn't work for all the volunteers, and even for the ones where it did work, it wasn't concentrated enough. They didn't know what to do, but this miracle cure was so important they thought of taking the cells where it was working, and growing them into whole human beings, because then all the tissues in the clone's body would have the cure in them.'

'Yes. That's more or less it . . . Tay, things were different then. If we were faced with the same situation today, of course we'd have tried to find another solution. But I don't know if we would have succeeded. Gene-therapy is very tricky, even now. There were seventeen of us, middle-aged volunteers. Fourteen of us had the M-389 result, in a rare kind of cell. We realised – something that people are realising again now, after forgetting about the idea for years – that the whole combination of an individual's genes can be crucial to the way a medicine works. We had a customised cure on our hands, and it seemed to us that the only way to go was to create more individuals of this crucial genetic type, with the change that we'd created in them. We weren't only working in preventive medicine, Lifeforce was also developing new bioproducts for *in vitro* fertilisation. Rei Chooi, she's called van der Hoort now, was confident that she could succeed with the nuclear transfer technique—'

'You knew it was dangerous, though.'

'We were ignorant and innocent and lucky, Tay. We thought of things, treatments and precautions, that the Welcare team rediscovered, to protect our human clones from development defects. We made sure the egg cell donor and the nuclear DNA donor were highly histo-compatible—'

Tay shrugged. 'I don't care. I don't want to live a long time. It doesn't matter, does it? Everyone I love is gone already.'

Pam stared at her with haunted eyes. 'I had never wanted children. I had friends instead. Ben and Mary Walker, and

Clint Suritobo. People like that were my family. Ben and Mary were so cut up when they couldn't have kids. I was very glad when . . . Is there anything you want to ask me? I mean, about the clone project?'

'Why are there only five clones, if there were seventeen volunteers? And why are we all different? Why didn't you make five the same?'

'Four of us dropped out, and in the end we could only find five birth mothers, who really wanted to have our babies, with good enough tissue matches. And it all had to be within the company, of course, because we were determined the children would be anonymous and live normal lives. But once we'd done that, everything else worked. We made five different clones because we weren't trying to mass-manufacture human beings, only to save something precious and amazing . . . and because each of you has a *different* genetic profile that produces the right antibodies. That was important, too. Tay, we took the law into our own hands. I don't know if what we did was right or wrong. But I can't be sorry that we did it, because now there's you—'

How could we be normal? Tay thought. How *could* we be?

It seemed to her that they both knew this wasn't the time to be talking about antibodies and clone ethics. But they couldn't either of them bear to talk about the real things.

Pam drew a breath. 'Tay, the clone project isn't really what I want to talk about. I just needed to make sure you knew enough, so that if you have to see yourself discussed in the papers or on TV there'll be no surprises. I really came to say . . . I want you to go back to Singapore.'

Tay's aunt Helen, her dad's sister, had flown out from England the moment she'd heard about the attack. She'd been in Singapore all this time. She wanted Tay to come and join her, and come back to England, to stay with her family. But Tay had refused to leave the Marine and Shore.

Tay felt the blood drain from her face. 'I don't want to go! You said I didn't have to go! I don't know Aunt Helen. She isn't even my real relative. I'm adopted!'

'This isn't about your aunt Helen. You don't have to go back to England. You can stay with the van der Hoorts. But you have to go. It's dangerous here, even if the army is winning, and you need to be away from this terrible suspense. You need people who can help you deal with your grief—'

'I have to stay and look after Uncle! What'll happen to him if I leave?'

Pam winced. 'Uncle will be fine, Tay. We're trying to find a new home for him.'

'You mean, another Refuge? It'll have to be somewhere we can be together—'

'Er, probably not another Refuge. That's not going to work, he's too old and, um, he needs special care. There are some big zoos, like the San Diego zoo in California, that have very good ape-centres—'

A shock of dread and horror went through Tay.

'A *zoo*! You'd put Uncle in a zoo?'

'He wouldn't actually be in the zoo, on display. An ape-centre means somewhere doing research. He'd have inter-esting things to do, and human company—'

'You can't send Uncle to a zoo!' cried Tay. 'He's isn't an animal!'

'All right, all right. Look, it's not going to happen right away. We can discuss—'

'*Don't* make me go to Singapore. I d-don't want to see a counsellor. I want to be here. Please, please let me stay. I have to be here until . . . until we know.'

They stared at each other. Pam started to reach out, as if to give Tay a hug. But her arms fell back. 'I won't make you leave,' she said. 'But I think you should. Really.'

After Pam had gone, Tay went down to Uncle's cabin. It was empty. The prisoner must be having his exercise. She walked in and sat on the bunk, and drew her legs up. The bedding was fresh, the cabin-cage was clean, but it smelled strongly of orang-utan. Uncle must hate that. The red apes don't live packed close together in huts full of their own smell, the way humans do. She knew how he must be feeling. Betrayed, betrayed . . .

Her throat was tight with the tears she refused to shed.

She sat there, her arms wrapped tight around her knees, a plan forming in her mind. There's the dinghy, she thought. Someone takes it to the shore every night, to get fresh grass and branches. I wouldn't have to launch one of the big boats. I can get food and water. And I bet I can get hold of the right keycard.

It was two in the morning when she left her cabin. She'd found her desert boots. They were very worn and battered, but they'd be better than bare feet. She had them slung around her neck. She'd collected a survival kit by wandering around the offices and the ship's galley, slipping things into her pockets. No one had stopped her; she was allowed to go wherever she liked. She'd had no trouble getting hold of the keycard either. She'd stolen it from Chen's jacket, when she was eating dinner with him and some of the other young technicians in the station canteen.

She was going to take Uncle home. They would make the same journey as they had done before, only in reverse. She could not make anyone believe that he was a real person, so this was the only solution. It would be morning before she or the ape was missed, and then the Marine and Shore would have to get official permission from the army to come ashore. By the time anyone came after them, Tay and Uncle would be far away. They could avoid the soldiers, of both sides. They would cross the savannah, cross the Waruk somehow, and then they would find a corner of the Refuge reserve that the fire had not touched; some patch of forest that nobody wanted. She imagined living there with Uncle, living off the fruits of the forest, among the wild things. But if she couldn't stay, if the humans tracked her down and dragged her back, at least they'd never find Uncle. He could escape into the high canopy, where humans couldn't follow.

The rubber dinghy with an outboard motor was kept tied up at the stern of the station. She peered over the rail, using the thin beam of her torch to make sure the metal ladder was in place. It looked a long way down. The motion would be strange, but Uncle wouldn't be afraid as long as he was with Tay. We'll climb down and cast off, and let the tide carry us, and then when we're well clear we'll switch on the engine.

She left her rucksack and her boots, and crept away to fetch Uncle.

There was someone with him constantly by day, but the ape was left alone at night, locked in. It was dreamlike and strange, sneaking down the dark passageway. The keycard opened the outer door, and the door to the inner cabin wasn't locked.

'Uncle?' she whispered. 'It's me, Tay. Come on, we're leaving.'

She switched on her torch, and found him, and took his hand. 'Nnh?' said Uncle. It was the first sound she'd heard him make since they reached the Marine and Shore, and her heart leapt. His hand gripped hers, warmly. She *knew* she was doing the right thing.

'Come on! Be very quiet!'

She had to tug him all the way, but he followed and kept quiet. They got out on deck, and made the long trek (it felt like miles) to the stern. She switched on her torch, and shone it so it lit her face.

'Uncle, I'm taking you home,' she whispered. 'We're going back to the forest.'

She turned the torch beam, so she could see his face, and was overjoyed to see that Uncle was *looking* at her, with expression in his eyes. With his free hand he gently stroked her face, making a very sad long-lip.

'Nnh,' he sighed. She knew he was saying, *we can't go back.*

'*Yes we can*,' hissed Tay. 'Trust me. Come on, we get over the side.'

She touched the top of the ladder; and then all hell broke loose.

Searchlights came on. Sirens wailed. Footsteps pounded. In seconds, Tay and Uncle were surrounded by the station's night-watch, all of them armed. In minutes, the whole staff and crew of the Marine and Shore seemed to have rushed to the spot.

'What the hell's going on?' yelled someone.

'I'm taking Uncle home!' shouted Tay, furious with herself for not having realised there would be people on guard. 'He hates it here. You can't keep him in a cage, he isn't an animal, he's a real person same as any of you, and you can't keep him like this.'

There was a mutter of amazement. Tay stood her ground, clinging to Uncle's hand. Pam Taylor came through the crowd, people making way respectfully as soon as they realised who it was.

'Tay . . . ? What are you doing?'

123

'I'm taking Uncle. We're going home. I won't let you send him to a zoo.'

'We won't send him to a zoo. Come on, come with me. We'll talk about this in the morning.' Pam put her arm around Tay. 'Okay, everyone can get back to bed, go back to sleep or whatever you were doing. No one is attacking the ship. Please, disperse quietly, I'll look after Tay and the ape.'

'HE'S NOT AN ANIMAL!' yelled Tay, throwing off Pam's arm. 'I'm taking him back to the forest. It belongs to him, not to humans! Uncle isn't a dumb animal! He has a right to be free. He's as intelligent as anyone, and you can't take his home away—'

While she was shouting, Dr Levier had appeared, and pushed his way to the front. The director of the Marine and Shore station was wearing a luridly-patterned batik dressing gown over green silk pyjamas, and carrying a large spanner. He looked furious. 'What are you trying to do to me, Pam?' he cried, waving the spanner. 'Am I in charge here or am I not? What is this upheaval? What does this young woman think she's saying? How long is this – this dangerous zoo animal going to stay on board?'

'I'm very sorry about the disturbance, Phillipe. Have some sympathy. Tay's been through a lot . . . and Uncle is not dangerous. He's as gentle as a lamb. Chen? Are you here? Please take Uncle back to his quarters.'

'He is NOT an animal!' howled Tay. 'You're saying that because Lifeforce did something. Lifeforce made him super-intelligent, and you're afraid people will find out. That's why he was so strange on the trek. That's why you want to send him away—!'

Pam's hand slapped, *crack*, across Tay's cheek.

Tay staggered back, holding her face, staring at her gene-mother in horror. Everyone else went very quiet. Chen came forward and took Uncle by the hand. 'Come on,' he said, in a subdued voice, 'come on, old boy, let's go.'

The crowd broke up. Pam got hold of Tay's arm, and marched her back to her cabin, sat her down on the bunk and shut the door. Tay set her teeth and glared. She felt stupid and childish and ashamed, but she wasn't going to show it.

For a moment Pam said nothing. She seemed to be forcing herself to calm down.

'Tay,' she said at last, quietly. 'You have to stop talking like that.'

'Like what?' demanded Tay.

'I am not angry with you. I understand what happened. I understand that you just want to go home, and there is no home for you to go to. You're desperate about your mum and dad and Donny, and I can't help you because I don't know how, and then I said you had to go to Singapore and leave Uncle. I don't blame you for trying to jump ship. It was my fault. I said the wrong things. I'm not used to being a mother. But you have to stop talking like that about Uncle.'

'What do you mean?'

'Saying he's not an animal.'

'Why do I have to stop telling the truth?'

'Because it's not the truth! Uncle was brought up by humans, and he's very different from a wild ape. He does things no wild orang-utan would think of doing. But he's an animal. Tay, don't you realise . . . ? This is a very dangerous situation for the apes. The People's Army rebels burned the reserve to get rid of foreigners. They're extremists. But there are ordinary people in Kandah, plenty of them, who think it's wrong that the orang-utans have, or had, a great big reserve of forest, that no one else was allowed to use. If word

125

gets out – and people do talk, even Lifeforce staff – that Lifeforce has "done something" to make orang-utans as intelligent as humans, if they think we want the apes to have human rights, what do you think will happen?'

'I don't know.'

'I'll tell you. The way things stand, we *might* get the reserve back, or another reserve. But we won't if the local people think we're putting the apes on a level with human beings. Do you want the orang-utans to lose one of their last protected homes? Is that what you want? Think before you speak!'

'You're trying to put me off,' said Tay coldly. 'But every word you say makes me more sure I'm right. You're trying to shut me up because I found out what Lifeforce did. Uncle is not a trained animal. He's a person, and you know it. I *told* you about the way he was. I told you about him talking to me, and reading—'

'Oh for God's sake. This is ridiculous. Lifeforce has done nothing to him.'

'You say that, but *you know I'm right*. Lifeforce made Uncle the way he is, and then dumped him in the Refuge, just the way you had me made, and then dumped me. I was bone of your bone, flesh of your flesh, but *you didn't want me*. You say you love me, but I know you're lying, because *I know you're lying about Uncle*.'

'Tay,' said Pam, in a different voice. 'I would not lie to you.'

'If I had to be a clone, why couldn't I be a wanted baby, even if I was only wanted to make my sister well? That would be better than being just an *experiment*. I'm not a girl to you. I'm an experiment like, like, FRANKENSTEIN'S MONSTER!'

Frankenstein's monster . . . Frankenstein's monster. Tay

126

felt as if she'd smashed through a great sheet of glass. She felt as if she'd vomited a great mouthful of poison. She had said it at last. She had said the words. Experiment. Monster. The cabin was spinning. Her arms and legs were shaking, she could hardly stand—

'All right,' said Pam, quietly and sadly. 'If that's the way you feel, I don't think there's anything I can say. I won't try to change your mind. But you must listen to me about Uncle. You were under enormous stress, and he was your only companion. He gave you all he had to give. But are you sure you're remembering things clearly? Don't torment yourself imagining things that aren't true.'

'I want you to get out of my room. If I'm allowed to be alone.'

'Goodnight, Tay,' said Pam. 'We'll talk in the morning.'

Tay had jumped to her feet when she was yelling. When the door had closed behind Pam, she took the blue pocket Shakespeare from the drawer of her bedside table and lay down on the bunk, hugging it to her chest. It was her talisman, her proof of the *reality* of what she believed. Maybe Uncle didn't read, maybe he had only turned the pages, but he was no different from a human being in his mind and feelings. She was sure of that.

But most of all, she was sure that Pam Taylor was lying.

Cold chills went down her spine. She had shrieked out the things she'd been thinking, but now the truth of it sank in. *Pam is lying to me.* She's never lied to me before, not about the clone project or anything, but she is lying about Uncle. I can feel it. I can feel it in my bones, in my heart—

So there's really something weird going on.

But that means Clint must have known, she thought.

And Mum and Dad. They must have known too. They must have been in on it. They betrayed Uncle too . . . Pam had told her that Lifeforce didn't want anyone to know that apes were as intelligent as humans.

Had Uncle been a mistake, then?

An experiment, like Tay. But an experiment that went wrong?

Her throat was tight with tears. Her whole world was crumbling.

I'm going to save him, I'm not going to let them dump him in a zoo.

But what power did she have?

It dawned on her that she *did* have power. She was one of the 'Lifeforce Teenagers'. If it was good for nothing else, being a Frankenstein's monster meant that people would listen to her. The idea made her grin in bitter triumph. She could talk to journalists, she could get on TV. The whole might of Lifeforce Biotech might try to crush her, but they wouldn't shut her up . . .

But something, or rather someone, made her stop and think. Someone so much a part of her that she could hear his voice. It was Dad's voice, and he was saying *don't oversteer*. A car will drive straight along a straight road. Don't haul on the wheel. Find out more, prepare your case before you open your big mouth.

Good advice, Dad. Even if you *were* a traitor . . . But how do I find out more?

Get into the Lifeforce computer system, said the voice; and investigate. You're Ben and Mary Walker's daughter, you are one of the five clones. Nobody will stop you from poking around, if you do it quietly and don't let anyone guess why you're doing it.

The next morning, she made no apologies. She thought

that might look suspicious. But she told Pam that she'd realised she needed help. She would go to Singapore, and see the Lifeforce counsellor.

Five

A helicopter came to the Marine and Shore for Tay. She took with her only her rucksack, holding a few borrowed clothes, the tattered pocket Shakespeare, and a piece of yellow blanket. Pam was there to say goodbye, trying to make peace and saying this was for the best. Tay gave her a brief, polite hug. As the helicopter rose she looked back and saw the coast of Kandah unfolding and spreading until she could see across the savannah to the dark green tapestry of the forest, where the smoke of more fires lingered. Maybe this was another goodbye, maybe she would never return – but for the first time in many days her face didn't feel stiff and tight from the effort of not crying. She had a reason to go on living. She had a mission.

I can't get you away from them myself, Uncle, she thought. Lifeforce is so much bigger than me. But I will find out the truth, and I'll find some way to tell the world.

She was to stay at Rei van der Hoort's house, which was an old Chinese mansion near the big wild park at Bukit Timah, in the centre of the island. Aunt Helen was there to meet her when she arrived. They had tea together – Tay and Aunt Helen, and Rei, and Rei's husband Matthis, who was a banker, a big, quiet man with a kind smile. Everyone made polite conversation – as well as people can, when the thing that has brought them together is something so terrible.

After tea Rei showed Tay and her aunt to the room that would be Tay's, and tactfully left them alone. It was a lovely room, cool and airy, decorated in rose and green, with a high ceiling, and a balcony overlooking the garden. Slatted shutters kept out the sun, but the glass doors to the balcony were open.

'Are you staying here as well?' asked Tay awkwardly. She wasn't sure.

Aunt Helen was a pale, earnest woman, dressed in summer holiday clothes that didn't suit the shocked and solemn expression fixed on her face. 'No, dear. The company's put me up in a very nice hotel. Taylor, I am so *very* sorry. I want you to know, your home really is with us. Your uncle, and Lewis and Marcie, are all agreed. I'd like you to come back to Southampton with me right now. I mean, as soon as we can arrange it.'

Lewis and Marcie were Tay's cousins, both of them older than Tay. She'd met them twice. Once on a three-week holiday in England (which she and Donny had both hated), and another time that she didn't much remember, years ago, in the days when the Walkers had lived in Geneva.

'I can't leave until I know what's happened to Mum and Dad.'

'Of course, dear. I know how you feel. But we'd be in constant touch, and you could come out East again straight away as soon as there was any news. It's not as if money's a problem . . .' Her voice trailed away, her eyes looked very sad. Tay guessed that Aunt Helen had been told that there was little hope that Ben and Mary were still alive.

'I'd rather stay.' Her face was feeling stiff again. 'Until I know for sure.'

Aunt Helen came over and took Tay's hands. 'It doesn't make *any* different to us, that you are . . . you know, a special test-tube baby. Mrs van der Hoort told us all about it and it doesn't matter. You're Ben and Mary's daughter as far as I'm concerned. We want you with us. We'll look after you, and give you a normal life. You can go to school with Marcie, you'd be in the year below her—'

'Thanks,' said Tay. 'I'm very grateful, I truly am. But I don't want to decide anything right now. Rei says I can stay here for as long as I need.'

Aunt Helen mopped her brow, and looked at the shuttered balcony doors with a little shudder. 'It's not the heat,' she said. 'It's the humidity. I'd *never* get used to this humidity, it drags me down . . . Well, I suppose you will be all right here, for the moment. I must say, the company does have a responsibility to you, poor girl. Don't you think you should close those windows? There are all kinds of nasty bugs out there.'

'I'll shut my windows at night. Thank you for everything, Aunt Helen.'

At dinner the atmosphere was more normal because the van der Hoorts' children were there: Sabine, the oldest, who was Donny's age, and Hans and Rikki, the seven-year-old twins. They were subdued, out of respect for the awful events in Kandah, and because of Donny, but they weren't completely solemn. Tay found out that she wasn't the only guest at the house. Another boy, a slightly-built, dark-haired boy of about her own age appeared, ate very little and slipped away without having said a word.

'Who was that boy?' she asked Rei, when Aunt Helen had gone back to her hotel.

'That's Taki,' said Rei, in a reserved tone. 'He's staying with us for a while.'

Tay took a wild guess – although not so wild really, seeing that the strange boy looked about fourteen, and a top Lifeforce executive was involved.

'Is he another of . . . ? Is he like me?'

'Yes,' Rei sighed. 'Trouble upon trouble. There are our people in Kandah, and their families – here, there and everywhere – and there's you and Taki, both needing help, so that I'm . . . I'm beginning to think Pam was right. We should have come clean from the start.'

'Pam didn't want the clones to be a secret?'

'She thought we should have told the world when you were born. She said that way the fuss would be over by the time you were old enough to care.'

'I don't understand why you didn't tell the world,' said Tay. 'Why do something so spectacular, and keep it a secret?'

'I was born in Japan, Tay, but I am half-Korean. I know how hard it is for a child to be an outsider. We didn't take the step we did for publicity. We had a duty to protect you.'

'I'll always be an outsider.'

'Not in my house,' said Rei, and Tay saw that there were tears in her eyes. Rei, too, was haunted and struggling with grief. 'Here, you are family.' But then she frowned, and laid a hand on Tay's arm. 'Tay, I must ask you. Has anybody asked you this? Did Clint give you anything to take away from the Refuge? He may have given you a disk? Or he may have hidden something? It's very important. Do you remember?'

Tay shook her head. 'No. He didn't give me anything.'

In the morning, Tay slept late. When she came down, the staff in the kitchen gave her breakfast. They told her a car would take her to town for her counselling session, and

133

meanwhile she could call Rei at work if she needed anything. She went out to the verandah at the side of the house. The boy who had slipped in and out of the dining room last night was there, with a laptop computer open on the rattan table in front of him. He looked up.

'Hello,' she said. 'I'm Taylor Walker.'

'I know,' said the boy, 'Rei told me. I know why you are here. I would offer my condolences, but I fear you must be tired of hearing that people are so sorry.' He spoke good but odd English, like someone in an old-fashioned book.

'Rei told me you were called Taki.'

'Takami Three Abe. Please tell me, do you play fantasy games?'

'Oh . . . Well, yes I do. I love Final Fantasy VII. I've played eight and nine too, but Seven was my favourite. I thought the Cloud Strife story was brilliant.'

Taki smiled, which changed his pale face a lot. 'Me too. I love the older games, and have a great desire to be a hero with a mysterious past. That is my test question, by the way. I believe only people who play fantasy games truly understand life.'

Tay sat down, and they talked about computer games. It was surprising how much they found to say to each other. Slowly, they got on to more personal topics. What does it mean to be a clone? Taki was like Tay. He'd never met the other clones. He had lived his life as a normal boy, going to an ordinary day school in Tokyo.

'But why are you here now?'

'I tried to kill myself,' said the boy, in a matter-of-fact tone. He looked Tay in the eye, then lowered his glance. 'I can imagine how that must sound to you. I know your story. How you suffered the death of people you loved, and fought to survive.'

He was wearing a long-sleeved shirt. She had not noticed before, but now she could see the edges of bandages on both his wrists. She didn't know what to say.

'W-what made you do it? Was it because the clone story was made public?'

'No. It had started before. Some people had found out, or guessed, from studying the M-389 results, what Lifeforce must have done. They had located me, and were sending me e-mail messages saying I should not exist. I was so ashamed, and I am a weak person. I didn't tell my parents, because I knew it would make them very unhappy. I told no one, until it got so bad I decided I couldn't go on. But my gene-brother had a bad feeling. He called my parents from California, where he is working. They found me in time to save my life, and then I came here, to be away, and think about my future.'

'Your gene-*brother*?'

'That's what I have called Takami One, now that I know him, since I was told the whole truth. We are agreed; he can't be my father. I have a father. He is like my identical twin, only so much older . . . Is it like that with you and Pam Taylor?'

'I don't know,' said Tay. 'I've never thought about it like that.'

In her worst despair, she had *never* thought of killing herself, either.

'Are you sorry you're still alive?' she blurted out.

'No,' said Taki. 'I feel as if I was an idiot. But I feel changed. My gene-brother was with me, and we talked. He's gone back to California now, and I will go home soon. But I think I might start at the Inheritors College, in Canada, next term, instead of waiting. I think that's where I most belong.'

The Inheritors College was another Lifeforce project, an

international college that the company had founded, and partly financed. It was the place where Tay had thought she would go when she was sixteen.

She nodded. 'Why *Takami Three*? What does that mean?'

He raised his eyebrows. 'Don't you know your number?'

'I don't know what you're talking about.'

'Then I won't tell you. You'll have to find out. Would you excuse me? I'm writing something, and I have to concentrate.'

He bent over his keyboard. Tay went back to her room. She tried to write a shopping list (she needed so many things). She thought about living in Southampton, under the cold grey skies of England . . . but mostly she stared out into the garden, thinking about her life, and about the strange Japanese boy who had wanted to die. Someone else like herself, someone who knew what it was like . . . But Taki was a Lifeforce kid. Even though he'd tried to kill himself, he still felt part of the company. He didn't know that Lifeforce was a sham. He didn't know that everyone he most trusted, even Rei van der Hoort, was involved in something hateful.

The driver came to fetch her. Rei had thought the counsellor ought to come to the house, but Tay had insisted she'd prefer the sessions to happen somewhere impersonal. The whole point of coming to Singapore was to have an excuse to be inside Lifeforce Asia's headquarters. The counsellor, whose name was Dr Rosetta Soo-yin, had an office on the forty-sixth floor of the shining, gold-glass Lifeforce Asia tower, near Keppel Quay. It was a spacious room, with a desk and filing cabinets at one end, paintings on the walls, and a sofa and armchairs by the windows overlooking the city. Tay found herself sitting in a peach-coloured chair, facing a small, plump woman in a smart suit and a ruffled blouse. She would have to pretend she wanted to be here, because otherwise the sessions wouldn't go on. But how do you talk to a counsellor?

'Don't worry, Tay,' said Dr Soo-yin. 'I know you don't really want to be here. You're doing it to please people. We'll see how it goes, eh? I will ask you questions, and you will try to answer – if you feel like answering. That will give a structure to the session, and make the time go by. Maybe, when you know me a little, you will want to talk.'

'Okay,' said Tay, cautiously.

They started off with very obvious things, that the counsellor must already know. How long had the Walkers been in Kandah? Did Tay like living in the forest? Tay couldn't bear to talk about the Refuge, or Mum and Dad, and talking about Donny choked her up, so she just answered 'yes' and 'no'. It was easier when they moved on to the future. She didn't mind telling the doctor that she didn't like England, that it was cold and grey and she didn't feel connected to her (adopted) relatives there. They got round to Tay's shopping list. There were so many ordinary material things that she had lost when the Refuge was destroyed. She would have to replace them.

'I'm going to need some money,' she confessed. 'I haven't asked Rei yet, but I only have a few dollars in my pocket-money bank account. I know I have a trust fund – does that mean I can get some cash now?'

'I don't think that will be a problem, Tay. Did no one ever explain the money to you?'

'Well, yes, Mum and Dad did . . . I know I have money, a lot of money, for later. But if it was, like, payment for being a clone, I didn't want it. So I never paid attention.'

Her face had started to feel stiff and tight. She'd thought

she was safe, talking about shoes and towels, a hairbrush and a new phone. But now she was seeing the Refuge clearing the way it had been after the fire, all burned, looking like an alien planet, and remembering the Walkers' ordinary belongings, those innocent helpless *things*, all gone. Dad's breakfast mug, Mum's clothes, the tree-frog Donny had made—

She stared at the carpet, her face stiff as a wooden mask.

'Tay,' said Dr Soo-yin gently, 'I know it hurts very much. And I know that you are a strong, brave girl, and you will conquer this pain, just as you conquered all the dangers and the ordeals of your escape. You have done so well. Everyone you know, everyone who cares for you, is very, *very*, proud. But listen to me, because I am older and maybe I know something about sorrow. If you fight and conquer the pain, you could be the loser in that victory.'

'I don't know what you mean.'

'There's something I want to suggest, and it is *only a suggestion*. There's a medicine I can prescribe, because as well as being a psychologist I am a doctor—'

'I don't want tranquillisers. Or sleeping pills. I'm all right.'

'It's not a tranquilliser, or a sleeping pill. It's something that will very specifically soothe your painful memories. You will be able to feel the grief, which is not your enemy, without becoming overwhelmed and confused—'

Tay was suddenly on her guard. She had noticed the word *confused*, at once. Confused is what they say when they mean somebody's mad, and having delusions.

'Has someone been telling you what I said about Uncle?'

Dr Soo-yin's prettily made-up face did a quick double-take. Very quick; but Tay saw it. 'Uncle?' she said. 'Ah, you mean, Uncle the orang-utan? The Refuge mascot? I know he was with you. A truly faithful friend, and a great survivor, like you, Tay. But why do you ask? What should anybody have told me about Uncle?'

'I wondered if someone might have told you I said he behaved like a human being.'

'Well, the red apes are highly intelligent. Maybe more than anybody knows, because we are social animals and they are not, and their intelligence is not what we recognise. This was Clint Suritobo's area of study. I've heard him talk about it, it was fascinating. Your parents were also very experienced—'

'I know,' said Tay. She looked up, her expression as innocent and unsuspicious as she could make it. 'Dr Soo-yin, I don't mean to be ungrateful, I know I'm meant to stay for an hour, but could we stop now? I'll make an appointment, and come back another time.'

Dr Soo-yin didn't look offended. 'Of course. The session is for you, not for me. But don't give up too easily. Maybe we will talk for longer next time.'

They agreed that Tay would come for another meeting in two days' time. Tay said she would think about taking the 'memory-soothing' drug. She was just about to leave when the doctor said, as if casually, 'Tay, there's one question. Excuse me, but, Clint was with you, wasn't he, all the time at the beginning of your escape?'

'He saved our lives.'

'Did he . . . did he give you anything to carry? Or maybe take something important with him, and hide it from the rebels?'

'No,' said Tay, blankly. 'We took food and water. There was no time, and Clint was hurt. We didn't think about anything else.'

She left the counsellor's office feeling very shaken. First

139

Rei, and now this counsellor woman. So they're all in on it, she thought. They've got it all worked out. They're going to give me a drug to destroy my memory of what really happened, and if I tell anyone about Uncle before they get me drugged, Dr Soo-yin is going to say I'm crazy.

And they want Clint's notes.

She was shaken; and she was angry.

Confused? When the van der Hoorts were being so nice to her, she'd been confused. When she'd walked into the familiar lobby of the Lifeforce Asia offices, where she'd so often met Mum and Dad, *then* she'd felt confused. But she wasn't at all confused now. She called the lobby, with a message for her driver saying there was no need to wait for her. She was going shopping and she'd take a taxi back to the van der Hoorts'. Then she took the lift to the forty-first floor, which housed Conservation Projects.

She had lied to Dr Soo-yin, and to Rei. They were right: Clint *had* insisted they take a package with them when they left the Refuge. Unfortunately, Clint's precious package was most likely at the bottom of the Waruk river. But, however important those notes were, they couldn't be the only evidence. An experiment that had given an orang-utan human intelligence had to be bigger than that. There must be something recorded on the computer system. She didn't expect to uncover the whole thing. All she needed was a hint of proof: a sign that there was something secret and weird going on—

She was alone in the lift. When she stepped out it was worse than walking into the lobby downstairs. Left from the lifts and then right by the big weeping fig in its planter . . . and here was the corner room that had been Mum and Dad's office since Tay was seven. There was a joke about orang-utans, a tatty newspaper cutting, still taped up on the

140

door. How many hours had Donny and Tay spent hanging around this floor, squabbling because they were bored, running races up and down the corridors? How many times had the four of them gathered for a rushed meal, before the flight home, among heaps of books and files, eating Hokkien food out of cardboard takeaway boxes—

She could not bear it. She backed away from the door as if it had demons behind it.

Clint's office was down the corridor. The door was still adorned with a sketch of a sombrero smoking a cheroot. It was locked, of course.

That was okay. Today she was simply proving that she could wander around and nobody would stop her. The next question was how to get hold of a keycard. Footsteps came along the corridor behind her. She turned, and saw an untidy young woman clutching a stack of tatty plastic folders. On the Conservation Projects floor nobody dressed to impress.

'Oh,' said the young woman. 'Is it Tay? You don't remember me? I'm Lucy, Lucy Hom.' She grinned. 'General dogsbody-person. Tay, I'm so very sorry. We're all just trying to hope . . . Well, Rei told me you might drop by. Do you need anything?'

'N-not really. I was here to see the counsellor and I thought of looking around the old haunts. I wondered if m-my mum's plants needed watering.'

'Okay,' Lucy handed Tay the stack of folders, and hunted in her bag and her pockets. 'Here's a keycard for the Refuge offices. I don't have a copy of the one for your mum and dad's room with me, but this will do. I'm sorry, it might be messy. I've been looking after the plants, but we haven't touched anything, not since . . . Not even the cleaners. Oh, Tay, I'm *so* sorry. It's awful, this waiting. Awful. Look, if you want to . . . ? If you'd like to have a soda with me, any time, and not talk about the bad stuff?'

'Yes,' said Tay, taking the keycard. 'Maybe. Um, thanks.'

Lucy hurried on. Tay decided she'd done enough for one day. She could not face opening Mum and Dad's office door.

Late that evening, after dinner, Tay lay on one of the rattan couches on the verandah at the van der Hoorts' house. Rei and her husband were indoors, the children were in bed. She was pretending to read, and trying to think.

She had believed in Lifeforce. Even after they'd told her she'd been made in a lab, as an experiment, like Franken-stein's monster, she'd still managed to think they were good people. But the evidence against them was too strong now.

They had made Uncle into something more than an animal. Why would they do that? Probably for no reason, probably just to see if they could. Then they'd kept him around, so they could observe his behaviour . . . but now, because of what had happened to the Refuge, they were in danger of being found out. They'd given a great ape the mind of a human being, and people would be *horrified* if that came out. So they were going to send Uncle to a zoo. Knowing that he had a human mind. Knowing that he could tell no one, and that he would be treated like an animal for the rest of his life.

How could they be so cruel? How could *Clint* have done something like that?

The worst horror was that Mum and Dad must have known something. But she was trying not to think about that. Of course, Pam had known everything. Pam and her guilty conscience had given the whole thing away. Because you can't lie to your second self.

They didn't think of that, thought Tay. They didn't realise I would only have to look at Pam Taylor, my gene-mother, and I would know that she was lying. I thought I was a copy of an extraordinary, brave, good person. I thought I was part of something important. I thought I was going to be one of the guardians of life. Instead I'm a human photocopy of something worthless.

Takami was on the verandah too, working on his super-duper Japanese laptop. To escape from her thoughts, she started watching the screen over his shoulder. He must be writing a program. There was nothing to see except lines of words and symbols.

Suddenly Taki gave a little chuckle. The laptop screen cleared. Two thin beams of light shot out from the tiny webcam eyes on the top rim of the screen. They meshed, while an image appeared on the dark screen. Held between the rays of light, the image grew and started spinning: a vivid green blob that separated into lobes like the segments of an orange, and then each segment burst into shining drops that danced around each other, like spinning chips of emerald.

'Hey, that's wonderful!' said Tay.

'It would be better with 3D glasses,' said Taki modestly. 'But I'm happy it works.'

'It looks like a swarm of fireflies.'

'Oh . . . It's meant to be a weapon, for the hero in my game.'

The emerald star-flowers were swimming in the night. Tay's heart gave a painful leap. Where had she heard that? Where had she seen the emerald stars? Oh yes . . . On the beach by that stream, when Donny had first been ill. She had woken in the night to find her little brother sitting up beside her, gazing at the fireflies. Donny had woken because he had a fever, but he had turned to her, with such a

143

beautiful light in his eyes, and he had said, '*How unbelievably great to see that—*'

My little brother Donny. He was so brave. He was such a brilliant kid.

'I've seen something just like that,' she whispered, aloud. 'When we were on the run, and my brother Donny was very ill. We saw a swarm of fireflies, one night.'

Taki turned round, leaving the program to run.

'What was he like, your little brother?'

'He . . . He had black hair and blue eyes, like Mum. He was nearly as tall as me. He wasn't terrifically good at things like reading and writing and maths and science, but he was good at art. And he was just brilliant fun. He was just, my best friend.' She looked at the neatly folded white cotton handkerchief that had suddenly appeared in her hand.

'What's this for?'

'Because you're crying.'

'Oh.' She wiped her eyes. 'You see, we lived in the forest, and it was a wonderful place to live. Sometimes people visit the rainforest and they say it's boring. You do see animals. You see the gibbons, and you see birds, and masses of butterflies, and monkeys sometimes. There were otters in the creek near our clearing until it dried up, and there was a mouse-deer, but it was very shy. But it's not like a wildlife safari. Usually, it's just the trees. Trees, and creepers, and big plants growing under them, and it's very silent. But it's not boring; it's subtle. It grows on you. You never want to be anywhere else.'

She wiped her eyes again, but the tears kept flowing. 'I loved the silence. I used to walk out, off the path, where the ground was clear, and sit down and just *be*. Oh, and there were the apes. You think you know the apes, when you've watched them for years. I thought I knew. But I didn't, until I was alone with Uncle.'

'This is the orang-utan who was your faithful friend?'

Tay shook her head. 'No. He was not my friend, and he was more than my friend. He was himself. It was, what Mum and Dad always used to say. A privilege. A privilege to be near them, because *they are like us*. They don't talk, but you can feel, there's a person, a different kind of person, with a mind but not like yours. It's like nothing else in the world. I can't explain.'

'I think you explain very well.'

Tay nodded, and scrubbed her eyes. She swallowed hard. 'I think,' she said, 'that someone who says he's weak, and can say that right out loud, and takes – takes responsibility for what he's done, probably isn't weak at all. He's probably very brave.'

'Thank you,' said Taki. He closed down his program. The laser beams and the green swarm disappeared. 'I will go to bed now. Er, please keep the handkerchief.'

It was a sodden grey lump.

'Thanks.'

Tay stayed on the verandah for a while, listening to the insect sounds in the garden, the 'nasty bugs' Aunt Helen had hated, that were the sound of home to Tay. Then she went up to her room. Before she got into bed she looked in the bottom of her rucksack, and brought out a tattered piece of yellow blanket. It had been washed, so it didn't smell of the terrible journey. But when she pressed it to her tear-stained cheek, she had a feeling as if tendrils of some kind were growing out of her, and reaching back: fragile tendrils that could easily be broken, joining her to the Tay who used to be, so she could be a whole person again. She fell asleep, cuddling Donny's blanket in her arms.

In the morning there was a square white envelope on the floor outside her bedroom door. There was a computer disk inside, and a note written on the outside, in clear black handwriting. 'Here is a copy of Emerald Storm, which I have renamed "Firefly Swarm". I am going home to Tokyo, but I think we will meet again, brave Tay. Taki.'

Tay went shopping with Lucy Hom, and (having bought a swimsuit) went swimming in the van der Hoorts' pool. It felt very luxurious, to be lying by the gleaming water, but she was sick with tension. And still there was no news.

Her second meting with the counsellor was the same as the first. Dr Soo-yin asked gentle questions. She said again that Tay should take the memory-soothing drug, and Tay said that she was still thinking about it.

'Dr Soo-yin, what if I wanted to see a counsellor who didn't work for Lifeforce?'

'Oh, well,' said the doctor, looking taken aback. 'Well, we could arrange that. But Tay . . . there is a difficulty. We'd have to tell them who you are. That you are one of the clones. It would not be fair to ask someone to try and help you, and keep something so important from them. Maybe, right now, that wouldn't be such a good idea.'

'I was just asking,' said Tay.

She took the lift down to Conservation Projects. Her mouth was dry and her palms were sweating. She was afraid she'd made Dr Soo-yin suspicious. What would happen if they caught me? A big company like Lifeforce could hide a murder, easily. But if she backed out of this, she had nothing. Only a battered pocket edition of Shakespeare, in her rucksack at the van der Hoorts' house, that meant nothing to anyone except Tay and Uncle—

A few people passed her in the corridor, no one challenged her. She stared at her mum and dad's office door, pierced by a shaft of grief as clear and true as a laser beam. She knew they were dead. Some of the Refuge staff might still be alive, but Mum and Dad were dead. She knew that, in her heart. If only she could stop hoping!

She could not bear to go into that room. She went along the corridor, and used the keycard to get into Clint's office. She shut the door very quietly. The venetian blinds were closed at the windows; the air-conditioning was cool but not icy. Thin fingers of burning sun lay across the floor and across the shelves of books: weighty tomes on animal behaviour, mixed with a shelf of tatty paperback Westerns. A pack of cigarettes, his thin black 'cheroots', was still lying on the desk. And already there was a film of dust over everything. Already, it was like walking into a tomb. She remembered Clint with Uncle, taking pot-shots at tincans, in the rain. In her memory he seemed so alive. How could someone so alive be dead? How could someone she'd trusted be a villain?

She sat down at his computer. When the Refuge had been attacked, Mum and Dad had tried to send their records to Singapore . . . But Tay wasn't looking for *recent* records. She was looking for something about Uncle from long ago. Something that would say why he was different. She powered up the computer, and tried to open the file register. A window appeared, prompting her to enter Clint's password.

'Oh no,' muttered Tay. 'Stupid! Of course I'll need a password.'

Her fingers tensed on the keys, and she could feel a prickling of fear across her shoulder blades. She'd have to guess right, and quickly. She knew that if she entered three wrong passwords the computer system would send off an alarm to the network administrator. That wouldn't normally be enough to get anyone interested: people were always forgetting their passwords. But this alarm message would be coming from a computer that belonged to someone missing – believed dead. There were eight spaces for her to fill. Eight letters, or numbers, or a combination of letters and numbers.

It's not his birthdate, she decided. People aren't allowed to use birthdates. It'll be something very easy to remember, though, because Clint was a scatterbrain, and no one could get him to bother about security . . . It used to drive Mum mad. Eight spaces, eight letters. Tay thought hard for about half a second, and typed.

EASTWOOD.

The screen cleared. Right first time. She was into the file register.

Now this is serious, she thought. If I am right and Lifeforce is guilty, and they catch me prying, I am in real trouble. They won't let me have another counsellor . . . because they don't want anyone outside the company involved. They'll give me that drug. I'll forget everything that happened on the trek, and the last remains of Tay Walker will die. There'll be nothing left of me but the Lifeforce clone, the human photocopy.

But she would go on. She must go on.

She started searching. There were files and files and files. There were articles on ape behaviour going back for years. There were complete copies of Clint's books, with the titles giving his proper official name, which looked strange to Tay: Mohammad Yamin K. Suritobo . . . You couldn't imagine Dr Mohammad Yamin K. Suritobo wandering around in a poncho, pretending to be Clint Eastwood. There was a huge folder on the Refuge, with records for every orang-utan that had passed through Clint's care. She recognised the names of 'graduates' from years ago . . . She opened one of these files, and read a funny little note from Clint to himself, about an ape called Melissa, who had not liked humans, and who had stolen things. It said he didn't know Melissa's name for the psychologist at the orphanage, but he was sure it was something very rude, and he knew she would prosper in her future career, because she had a fine criminal mind. There was no record for Uncle, except a file with scanned documents in it, from the year when the Walkers had taken over the newly-founded Lifeforce Refuge. The documents covered his transfer from Sumatra, they said he was free of TB infection, and he was not to be released. At the end of the file there was another note from Clint to himself. It said: 'Uncle's whole story + video clips, filed with new book.'

Tay started to feel reckless and frustrated. There was nothing here, not a hint that Uncle was different from any other ape. She logged into the Lifeforce intranet, using the missing, believed dead man's password, to see how far EASTWOOD would take her. 'Okay,' she muttered, tapping in her query. 'My name's "Eastwood", and I want to look at *all* the secure files I can access, about anything to do with the Kandah Refuge. So there.'

It took time. Seconds passed. Then the screen cleared, and the results of her search came up as a long list of titles. Her eyes were irresistibly drawn to the startling mention of her own name. Taylor Five Walker.

Taylor *Five*? Taki was three, she remembered. What do the numbers mean?

But why was she getting documents about a teenage clone, when she'd asked about orang-utans? She clicked on one of the titles; and of course, the connection was the Kandah Refuge. She found herself reading a letter.

It wasn't really a letter. It was a file of old e-mails, from ten years ago. The kind of thing that gets stowed away on a big computer archive, like a box of papers in a corner of the garage, and never thought of again. Ben and Mary Walker to Pam Taylor, with Pam Taylor's replies. Tay began to read, scared and excited. These letters dated from the founding of the Kandah Refuge. The secret about Uncle *must* be in here somewhere . . . But Ben and Mary and Pam weren't talking about an orang-utan. They were talking about a little girl. A little girl that all three of them loved . . . How would the children feel about this move? Would Tay and her baby brother be happy in the forest?

She loves the outdoors, she's so fearless, and we want her to be *free—*

'I was,' whispered Tay, aloud, her tears falling fast. 'Oh, I *was*. I was happy—'

Something in her broke open, like light on darkness. She felt as if she'd been sleep-walking, and suddenly she was awake; as if she'd been completely out of her mind, without knowing it, and suddenly she was sane again. The trek, the Marine and Shore research station, the way she'd come to Singapore, it had all happened in a dark dream. Now the real world had come back, and she knew that the fears she'd had about Mum and Dad, and Clint and Pam and Rei, were utterly crazy.

How could she have doubted them? How could she have thought that Mum and Dad, her own mum and dad who loved her, and *Clint*, the kindest, most righteous person in the world, would have done anything to harm the apes? How could she have believed that they were involved in a plot to do anything cruel? Never!

The door behind her opened.

'Hi,' said Lucy Hom. She came and sat down, and gave

150

Tay a tissue from her pocket. 'I thought I'd find you in here. I knew you hadn't left the building, because you still have your security tag. I looked in your mum and dad's room—'

It seemed as if Tay had to spend her life taking handkerchiefs from people.

'Is it – is it news?' she gasped. 'Have they been found?'

'I'm sorry, no . . . It's not that. I have a satellite call for you from Pam, from the Marine and Shore. If you switch your phone on, I think I can patch it through. Pam needs you to go back. It's Uncle. Apparently he escaped. They don't know how, but he's disappeared.'

Six

The Marine and Shore research ship was back at its mooring, in a deep-water bay at the north-eastern tip of East Kandah. Tay's helicopter landed on the foredeck about noon the day after Lucy Hom had found her reading Clint's files. By the time she'd got the message, it had been too late to arrange a flight back out here. She could see Pam waiting for her. Tay had only been away a week, but she felt so different it was as if the world had turned upside-down. There was a fluttering in her stomach. She didn't know how she was going to face her gene-mother, after the way they'd parted; after the things Tay had said.

She was afraid for Uncle, and she was afraid for herself.

The helicopter touched down, and Tay waited for the rotors to slow before she got out.

'I hope you find him,' said the Singaporean pilot. 'You know, it would mean a lot if we could know poor old Uncle was safe.' The Refuge mascot's story had become important to people at Lifeforce Asia. People who had friends and colleagues among the hostages, who were desperately waiting for news, like Tay and Pam, clung to the story of Uncle, the faithful orang-utan who had survived. Maybe the story of his miraculous appearance on the shore, and the way he'd led the rescuers to Taylor Walker, had become a little exaggerated, but that was understandable. People tend to exaggerate anything that helps in a bad crisis.

Pam stood waiting, with Chen, the technician who'd been Uncle's chief babysitter.

'Is there any news?' said Tay. It was the question everyone had been asking, all the time, since the attack on the Refuge. *Is there any news?* But this time it meant Uncle.

'No,' said Pam. 'Come inside; we'll tell you what happened.'

She didn't try to hug Tay, and hardly even smiled. She just led the way to her office on the upper lab deck. As they walked through the lab, Tay saw the brittle stars were still waving their tinsel arms in their row of tanks; and she had the strange feeling that she was coming home. Her lonely journey through the wilderness had not been over, when she arrived at the Marine and Shore station the first time. Now, maybe, it was nearly at an end. But only if Uncle was safe . . .

The three of them sat down. 'It was my fault,' began Chen, looking miserable. 'I'm *so* sorry, Tay. You see, I was trying to help him. I thought he was tame, fixed on human company. He seemed so docile, so quiet. I didn't know he would—'

'Let's start at the beginning,' Pam broke in. 'The day after you left, the army lifted the restrictions on our position. We were allowed to move back to our mooring. As soon as we'd made the move, and reoccupied the shore camp, Chen wanted to get Uncle on solid ground again and I agreed. It was a good idea.'

'We made a home for him in one of the storage huts,' explained Chen. 'We rigged up an open run in front of it. There wasn't a padlock on the gate to the run, but it was roofed over. And there was a secure catch. Some of us were sleeping on shore; he wasn't there by himself. He was still pining, but he seemed happier.

'We took him out and let him wander around, in the daytime, but we kept him on the collar and lead. Of course, he was loose, at night, in his run and his sleeping quarters. Yesterday morning, I took him his breakfast, and he was there okay. An hour later I came back, the run was open, and Uncle was gone. I thought someone had taken him for a walk. I really didn't think he could have escaped. I went around looking for him, asking people. I called the ship, to see if someone had taken him back on board. It was a couple of hours before we knew he was gone. He must have opened the catch somehow, and climbed the perimeter fence—'

'We searched the area,' said Pam. 'We couldn't find him, but we were sure he wouldn't have gone far. We waited, but he didn't come back. When he'd been missing overnight, I decided we had to send for you.'

'He's microchipped,' said Chen. 'We can identify him if we find him. We'll know him from a wild animal, even if he doesn't know us. But that's not much use. If only we'd thought to put a radio tracer on him. We could have done that, easily; we do it to marine mammals all the time. But we never imagined he would run away!'

'We can identify him anyway,' said Tay. 'He'll be the only orang-utan on the savannah, it isn't their country. And he doesn't look a bit like a Borneo ape.'

'That's good!' said Chen, looking doubtful. He had done his best for Uncle, thought Tay. But he was a Marine and Shore technician, he didn't really know anything about the red apes. 'I shouldn't have left him,' she whispered. 'I *knew* I shouldn't have left him. I was the only one who knew about orang-utans. It was my job to look after him . . . It's not your fault, Chen. I'm the person who let Uncle down.'

'Well, you're here now,' said Pam. 'With your help, I'm sure we'll find him. I want you to come out with me into the savannah, Tay. We'll take a Land Rover, and go to where we picked you up when you arrived here. The chances are he isn't far away. There are trees, there's long grass, he's smart. He could be hiding, watching us search. If he sees you, he might decide to show himself.'

'Maybe I should come along?' offered Chen. 'He knows me best of all the crew. We'll need a net, and a dart-gun, if he comes near; and you'll need help.'

Tay and Pam looked at each other. *He means well*, said their glance. 'No,' said Pam, 'we won't go after him with a net and tranquilliser darts, not yet. We'll try to get him to trust us again, and believe that we're his friends. That would be best.' She was looking at Tay as she spoke, smiling sadly.

Tay felt herself blushing.

'Come on,' said Pam. 'Let's go. He's been missing for two days, and there isn't much water out there. Or much that an ape would eat. We have a few hours of light left.'

The Marine and Shore station was linked to the beach by a bridge of floating pontoons. Tay and Pam crossed over; Chen came with them. He showed Tay the run the crew had made. It had been put together with care, and roofed over with panels of heavy wire mesh; but the catch on the gate was pathetic. It wouldn't have puzzled a monkey, never mind an orang-utan. Some of the shore-camp staff came hurrying to greet Tay, and tell Pam how things were going. They'd been in touch with the East Kandah National Park headquarters; the people there were sending a tracker. But it was a hundred kilometres away, and every vehicle that moved on the road had to have an army escort—

We have to find him ourselves! thought Tay, dismayed. If

155

he sees people in uniform hunting him down, he'll never, never come near. He'll die out there—

They got into the Land Rover and drove out into the golden landscape, leaving the huddle of huts and the perimeter fence behind them. Neither of them said a word, as Pam took their vehicle off the trail and they went jolting through the dry grass. At last she pulled up, in the shade of a half-starved acacia tree.

'Is this where you found me?' said Tay. 'I don't remember anything—'

'It's roughly the place. Tay, before we go any further you'd better tell me, do you still think we're looking for an ape with super-intelligence? A "human" ape?'

Everything that she'd gone through with Uncle on the trek was clear in Tay's mind, and everything was true, but it looked different now. So much had happened to her in those few days in Singapore. She had been with the kind van der Hoorts, doing ordinary things. She had met Taki, and she had read those old e-mails, which had made the world come straight again. She knew her memories of Uncle on the trek were genuine in some deep way. But they could not be trusted as facts: they were fever-dreams. She could understand now how mad she must have sounded, yelling *Uncle is a person*.

Claiming that Lifeforce had made a mutant, human-ape, who could talk and read, and for some unknown reason had kept this ape at the Kandah Refuge, for years, in secret.

'Why didn't you want me?' she said at last. 'I was bone of your bone, flesh of your flesh. Nothing can change the way I feel about Mum and Dad, but I was *your baby*. Why did you let Lifeforce take me away? Was there no room for me in your life?'

Pam didn't tell Tay that they were supposed to be talking about Uncle.

'You want to know that now? Well, I was fifty-three when I started taking M-389—'

Tay glanced at her, startled. There was grey in Pam's golden-brown hair. But Tay had always assumed her gene-mother was *younger* than Mum.

'Yes, fifty-three, and I was developing arthritis in my hands.' She lifted them from the steering wheel, and flexed her strong, tanned fingers. 'That's not a good thing for a lab scientist. It's gone now . . . I think it was wrong – women have to take the drugs, after all. But in those days, no one tested drugs on women of childbearing age. Like the other women among the M-389 volunteers, when we reached the point of deciding to make human clones, I was too old to bear my own child. Of course anything's possible now, but we didn't even consider the idea. But there was another reason, Tay. We were sure it would be wrong for the clones to be brought up by their own gene-parents. What would that be like? Having an identical twin for a parent? We thought it would be unbearable. I believed it was for the best. I wanted Ben and Mary to have you. But when I held you in my arms, for the first time, oh, it was very hard to let you go—'

'I think you never thought about the consequences. I think you never thought about how it would feel to be us. Me, and the other four clones.'

'Maybe we couldn't imagine that. What we thought of was . . . Diseases of the connective tissue. Degenerative diseases that attack the myelin sheath of nerve fibres. Autoimmune disease: all of these things. You know some of the famous names. Arthritis is one. The many variants of arthritis. Multiple sclerosis, muscular dystrophy. Transplant

157

rejection. Lupus. Scleroderma. I don't want to get too excited, but there are many more.'

'All right, all right . . . I know all that. When I was in Singapore I heard them saying on the TV, it was like discovering Penicillin.'

Pam nodded. 'Yes. It's like discovering Penicillin. We have a group of medicines that will not "cure" old age, but will dramatically improve the quality of our natural lifespan. It's been a long and difficult road, much more complex than we could have imagined when we made our rash decision, but we are there now. The tissue samples, the blood factors, from all five of you, have been used to develop cheap, effective treatments—'

'Is that why I'm rich?'

'Well, no. We made the M-389 antibodies open-source, non-profit-making. But we've made money out of other, less important things. You're rich because you're a member of Lifeforce, you have shares in the company.'

'It's always *Lifeforce*. Why do you let the company rule your life?'

Pam had been staring out through the windscreen. She turned and looked at Tay, with an expression that Tay had often seen in a mirror.

'Lifeforce is me, Tay. Don't you understand? Lifeforce is *me*. And Ben and Mary Walker, and Clint Suritobo, and Rei Chooi, who is Rei van der Hoort now; and some other people you've met, but you don't know so well. We started the company, twenty years ago. When Lifeforce turned into big business, Ben and Mary and Clint and I decided to branch out into conservation. Clint had always wanted to study ape behaviour, instead of testing drugs on them. That's how the Kandah Refuge project started . . . But before that, the clone idea was ours too. Oh, Tay, people talk about big faceless corporations being dangerous. But the faceless corporations have nothing on the danger of a small group of friends, with ambitions and ideals and a brand new science to play with. We thought we could do *anything*. We did something that should have been impossible, to keep hold of what we'd found in M-389 . . . I think we were mad to decide we could make human clones, so long ago, no matter what the benefits. But how can I regret what we did, when it gave me *you*?'

'I think *you're* the irresponsible teenager here,' said Tay. 'I think you are nuts.'

'You're probably right.'

They hugged each other, and in that hug a lot of pain was burned away.

'It was the book,' said Tay, when she let her gene-mother go. She knew that she'd been half out of her mind, but she felt she had a right to defend herself. 'Uncle was my friend, my guide, when I had no one. When I saw him on the ship I was so shocked. He was like a zombie. I thought he must be *pretending* to be a dumb animal, because he was afraid of you. And . . . there was my Shakespeare, in his cage. How could he have got hold of that? I'm *sure* I'd thrown it away, out on the savannah—'

'It was in your pack,' said Pam abruptly.

'Oh.'

'I gave it to him. That's the solution to the mystery. I couldn't bring Uncle to your cabin, while you were recovering those first two days, because of Phillipe's attitude. So I told him you were safe, as best I could; and I gave him something of yours. It seemed to comfort him.'

'Okay, but there was more,' said Tay. 'When I woke up on the Marine and Shore, you told me you *knew* I was with Uncle, because sometimes you know things about me. Like an identical twin . . . Well, when you told me Uncle was fine, I *knew* you were lying. I'm sorry, Pam, but I still feel it and I don't understand. I kept saying *Uncle's a person!* and you kept saying no, but *you were lying*. Or hiding something. I thought it must be something Lifeforce had done.'

'Uncle is a person,' said Pam, 'You were right.'

'What?' Tay was stunned. 'What do you mean?'

Pam sighed. 'I mean, simply, Uncle is a person. An orang-utan person. He didn't need to be treated with any weird drug to make him nearly human. He was born that way, like every orang-utan, like every one of the great apes. If you thought I was behaving like someone with a guilty conscience, that's because I do have a guilty conscience. Because the woods are burning, the apes are losing their homeland, and there's nothing I can do.'

'I know the forest is burning. It's *horrible*. I could see the fires from the air. I saw the satellite pictures of the whole of Kandah on TV in Singapore—'

'No, Tay. I don't mean what's going on now. The rebels are in retreat, and the fires of this summer will be controlled. I don't mean just the logging companies either, though they are part of it. I mean, nearly all the great forests of Borneo and Sumatra are gone already, and Kandah was our last stand. And though it's tragic how quickly, how crudely it has happened, it had to come. There are millions of people living on these two great islands, Tay. They want farmland, and space to live, and washing machines, and cars, and roads, and hospitals and schools. No one has any right to tell them, *you can't do it*. Of course there'll be reserves, and National Parks, where a lot of the fabulous wildlife will survive. But they'll be small, compared to the forest that was the orang-utans' home, and it won't be enough. They're solitary creatures, each of them needs a wide territory, and they aren't going to change their ways. Very soon there may be no wild apes left.'

'That's what Clint used to say,' said Tay. 'I won't believe it. Lifeforce is rich. You can campaign, you can tell the world, you can *make* people share . . . If you have a guilty conscience, if you care, why don't you do something?'

'Lifeforce made a lot of money very quickly, Tay. Now we're spending money on conservation and on education. But we're trying to spend it wisely. We want to help, but we're not martyrs to a hopeless cause. We don't fight battles we can't win.'

'What about the people at the Refuge? What about Mum and Dad? Didn't they die for something they believed in?'

'They died by accident,' said Pam, bitterly. 'Because I was stupid, and I didn't get them out of danger. They died for no reason; our loss won't help the apes.'

Tay almost wished the evil conspiracy had been real. It would have been easier to take than the bleak sadness in her gene-mother's voice and eyes. Grief ought to be dignified. When a tragedy happens, people ought to be kind and gentle with each other. But it doesn't always turn out that way. She took Pam's hand, wishing she could undo all the yelling and the upset of the last weeks; feeling again that rush of love. She no longer felt that Pam had to have the answer to everything. It's like Taki said, she decided. I have a twin sister, much, much older than me. But she's not *old*. She's not even a grown-up, not all the time. She's just Pam, and she needs me.

'Mum and Dad died doing the work they believed in,' she said, very firmly. 'That doesn't make them useless martyrs to a hopeless cause. They didn't mean to die, they weren't taking stupid risks. It was nobody's fault except the killers'.'

They looked at each other, each of them realising what

161

had been said. Hope would not die, not until the very end; but they had both admitted that they were sure Ben and Mary Walker were dead. They said nothing, they just gripped hands very tight.

Sometimes silence is best.

'It wasn't just Uncle,' Tay said at last. 'There were other things. In Singapore, the counsellor tried to get me to take a drug that would make me forget. I was sure she was trying to destroy my memories of Uncle being human . . . *And* she and Rei both asked me whether Clint had taken anything from the Refuge, something secret he'd maybe tried to hide. So then I thought everyone in Lifeforce was in on the plot—'

'Oh, boy . . .' sighed Pam. 'Well, I can explain. Maybe Rosie and Rei shouldn't have asked you – I'd already told them you hadn't brought anything with you . . . but the truth is, we *did* hope that Clint had managed to save some important notes. When Ben and Mary got through to Rei, when the attack was going on, they said he was going to try.'

'He did,' said Tay. 'He gave me a package. I didn't tell Dr Soo-yin, or Rei, because I thought they were the enemy. But it's gone. I'm sorry; we lost it. I think it ended up at the bottom of the Waruk.'

'Oh well, so that's that . . . We knew there wasn't much chance.'

'What about the memory-destroying drug? That was *very* creepy.'

Pam frowned, and looked guilty. 'I think you should take it.'

Tay stared at her, amazed and outraged.

'Don't look at me like that. Eumnesystin will not destroy your memories. It will break the loop that makes remembering hurt so much that you can't bear it . . . I watched you,

162

Tay. Physically, you recovered amazingly quickly, but that only made it harder. I saw you shutting yourself off, refusing to cry. I was sure you were starting to believe crazy things about Uncle as a way to escape from your grief. That's why I had to let you go—'

'I don't want it to stop hurting,' said Tay, fiercely. 'If it stops hurting, that means I've started to forget. I don't want to forget them. I'd rather go on hurting forever.'

'Then take the Eumnesystin. It will help you. The pain won't be a monster that you have to fight, or run away from. It'll be something you can accept. You'll be able to live with your grief. You'd take painkillers if you had a broken leg, wouldn't you?'

'Is that what the future is going to be like?' demanded Tay, disgusted. 'Emotions you can order like hamburgers? Hold the pickle, extra mayonnaise? Is that what you think I need? A pill to mend a broken heart?'

'I don't know what the future's going to be like, Tay. I'm talking about you, now. I want to help you, because I love you. I know I'm clumsy. I'm not your mum, I'm not your dad, I'm a crabby old scientist who never had any family except my friends—'

Tay had to look away, or she would have started crying again. For a while they sat in silence, holding hands. Finally, they both got out of the Land Rover. The Marine and Shore had run out of fresh fruit and vegetables days ago; the helicopter that had brought Tay had also brought fresh supplies. They dragged one of the boxes out of the back, and arranged a tempting pyramid of fruit – which instantly attracted a buzzing swarm of flies.

'If he's anywhere around, he's been watching us,' said Tay.

They waited, but Uncle didn't turn up. They drove to the

coastal waterhole, which was even smaller than when Tay and Uncle had passed this way. The mud was even more trampled and churned than it had been. Tay found two orang-utan footprints, but they were old and dry; she couldn't tell how long they'd been there. Above the dell, out in the open where it would be clearly visible, they set another offering of fruit.

'When I was in Singapore,' said Tay, 'I heard someone on TV say the "Lifeforce Teenagers" were "human pharm animals". Genetically engineered animals bred so their bodies will produce medicine. I suppose it's better than being Frankenstein's monster, made just for an experiment. I don't think Uncle's going to turn up here, either.'

They drove around until sunset, leaving caches of fruit and bottles of water. Tay knew that Uncle could easily deal with a screw-cap. But they both felt it was useless. They kept calling in to the shore camp: Uncle hadn't reappeared there, either.

'I think I know where he's gone,' said Tay, as they drove back to camp in the dusk. The feeling had been growing in her all day. Uncle was nowhere near. He wasn't hanging around, watching the humans from hiding. He was far away. 'This isn't his country; he can't live here. I think Uncle is trying to go home.'

After two more days of useless searching and waiting, a detachment of the Kandanese army arrived at the Marine and Shore camp. The Kandah River Region was in the army's control again. They were ready to recover Donny Walker's body, for a proper burial. Tay and her gene-mother set off with the soldiers, but in their own Land Rover, towards the Waruk river. They were still searching for Uncle, and the soldiers were eager to help. The Lifeforce mascot had become a symbol of peace and renewal. The cavalcade stopped frequently, and the soldiers fanned out on either side of the track, beating through the long grass. A helicopter, cruising in wide sweeps across the savannah, kept reporting to the land party by radio. Tay knew that all of this was completely useless. Uncle would never be found; he would never let himself be caught by people in uniform. He'd seen what had happened to Clint. But she said nothing. She knew where Uncle was heading. Her only fear was that he could not possibly have survived the journey. But orang-utans are tough. They're adapted for the trees, but in great need they can make long journeys on the ground. They can do without food or water, if they must, for at least as long as a human.

At Aru Batur the raft ferry had been repaired, but the village was still a smouldering ruin. It was dark by the time they'd crossed the Waruk. Tay and her gene-mother put up their tent on the edge of the soldiers' camp, on a patch of clear ground near the mosque. There'd been rain here, though the savannah was still dry as bone. Everything that had been burned was thick with wet ash and mud. People had been back to salvage what they could from the wreckage of their homes. There were trails of discarded clothes, shoes and broken household things, lying in the dirt between the abandoned houses. The sky above was thick and heavy, without a star or a ray of moonlight. The air was full of the choking incinerator smell Tay remembered only too well. One of the soldiers came over with a tray of rice and spicy mutton stew, and bowls of broth. Neither of them had much appetite, but they ate a little. They pasted themselves with insect repellent, and sat on the groundsheet in the mouth of their tent.

'I wish we could leave Donny where he is,' said Tay softly.

It was the families in England, Aunt Helen and her husband, the Walker grandparents, and the relations on Mum's side, who wanted Donny's body to be brought out. Tay had conflicting feelings. *Really*, she felt that it didn't matter. Donny would always be with her, whatever anyone did. But it was horrible to think of his body being taken from the grave of green branches and river stones that she and Uncle had made.

'I suppose the family has a right.'

Pam said nothing, she just put her arm around Tay's shoulders.

Tay noticed that there were hardly any insects dancing around their lamp. The fire had driven every kind of life away, even the tiny creatures. But they would be back. When a firestorm passes through, what isn't destroyed grows stronger.

'Pam? I know I'm called Taylor after you, but why am I called Taylor *Five*? I read that name when I was looking for evil secrets in Clint's files. And Takami Abe is Taki *Three*; but he wouldn't tell me why.'

By now, she had told Pam the whole story of her time in Singapore.

Pam sighed. 'Well . . . That's because . . . Our project wasn't like animal clone projects you've read about and heard about. We didn't make hundreds and hundreds of cloned embryos. We wouldn't have known how. We didn't have the technology. Every attempt was a major operation, a major emotional investment. With you, it was five. Five times we harvested my M-389 cells, which wasn't easy. And Mary's egg cells, likewise. Rei did the nuclear transfer, and we implanted the embryo. Four times, Mary was pregnant for a few weeks and we lost the baby, for one reason or another. The fifth time, it worked.'

'So . . . I had four beginnings-of-sisters, who didn't make it?'

'You could put it that way. We kept telling ourselves we had to go on, but it was terrible at the time. Every one of those pregnancies was a child, to us. But we carried on, and now there are five of you. I'm afraid you're going to have to bear some publicity, Tay. But it won't last long. There'll be another science news story along in a few weeks. If that's what you want, you can go back to England, and live with your Aunt Helen, and have nothing more to do with Lifeforce. Or me.'

'So I'd be Tay Walker, an orphan with a trust fund, not your daughter?'

'Mm. That's about it.'

'What do *you* want?'

Pam stared ahead of her. 'I want you to be happy, that's all.'

Tay said nothing. She listened to the noises of the night, and thought about the way that she had been made. It was weird to think that her cells, her M-389 altered gene-profile, had been the source of a medicine as new, and as powerful against disease, as Penicillin had once been. Human beings are supposed to *make* discoveries, not *be* discoveries . . . It's as if I'm a tree, she thought. Or a fruit, or an animal. She thought of the great forest trees, the guardians of life, that she had loved so dearly. The forest must be felled, but something new would be born. Something that would never replace what was lost. But there are always new things, she thought; and this time, something new was also a *someone*: a girl called Tay Walker, with all her memories and griefs and hopes and dreams. And this was life, good and bad so closely woven together. And this was science, too; the great romance of *finding out*, by accident or on purpose, stretching back through history, and reaching on ahead—

Correction, she thought. Not Tay Walker. Taylor *Five* Walker.

That's me. That's who I am.

In the morning they made their own breakfast: coffee and sweet rolls for Pam, juice and rolls for Tay, who didn't like coffee. The Kandanese soldiers were very friendly, but Tay couldn't talk to them. She flinched when they came near. With their camouflage fatigues and their rifles, they looked exactly like the rebels who had stopped Clint. Whenever she looked at them, she remembered the terrible look in the eyes of those other men, and she felt sick. The officer in charge knew she was the daughter of the orang-utan Refuge wardens, and he could see she was unhappy with the escort. He tried to reassure her.

'I hope you will love Kandah again, some day,' he said, in English. 'You will remember that this is a beautiful country, and you have been happy here.'

Tay shook his hand; but she didn't feel much better.

Now only thirty kilometres of dirt road and rough track stood between Tay and the place which had once been her beloved home. But they were not going to the Refuge clearing – though Pam would have to go there soon, when the search was made for the bodies of her friends. This time, they set out along the track that led from Aru Batur to the valley where Tay's brother lay. The farmhouse where Tay had looked for help and found none had been burned down, some time over the last few days. They drove past the blackened framework. Soon after that the track became too narrow for vehicles. Some of the soldiers stayed behind. The others, carrying a stretcher and other necessary things, kept their distance behind the young girl and the older woman – so alike in their jungle clothes, with their golden-brown hair, in the way they walked, in the set of their shoulders and the way they glanced around them, that they could have been twins of different ages. There were no more traces of the fire. Everything was green. They made their way along the bank of the clear, rippling water of the little tributary of the Waruk.

'Look,' said Tay. She pointed to a pale strip of tattered plastic, tied around a branch. It was one of the signs she'd left, on her way back from Aru Batur the second time. 'I put that there. I tore up a T-shirt and an old carrier bag that I'd picked up in Aru Batur market. I used the T-shirt first. The plastic means we're getting near.'

She looked ahead and saw, with a stab of mingled grief and tenderness, the river beach where she had spent her little brother's dying days. Where she had talked to Donny, and sung him the songs he liked best, and cuddled him, and laid him down to rest. The burial cairn was still there, covered in a heap of green branches.

The branches were fresh.

Tay stopped, when she saw that. 'Pam,' she said. 'I can't talk to the soldiers. Will you ask them to stay back? That's Donny's grave, and Uncle's here. I knew he would be.'

Pam spoke to the officer, then she and Tay went on alone.

They came to the cairn. Tay knelt on the pale sand. 'This is where he died,' she said, softly. 'We didn't move him. Uncle didn't want to move him, or bury him . . . Oh, I know it was me. I know I was m-making up that Uncle talked to me. But I remember it still, and what I remember about Uncle is *true*, inside. We couldn't save him. When I had to give him the morphine, I knew he was going to die.

169

On the last evening . . . well, I can't talk about it. He died, and we buried him, and look, Uncle's put green branches. He's made Donny a sleeping-nest, like a mother-ape looking after her baby.'

Pam Taylor touched her daughter lightly on the shoulder, and took a few steps back. She had seen movement in the green shadows of the valley-side. She crouched down and watched, keeping very still, as the rust red ape slipped out of the trees.

Let them mourn their dead in peace.

Tay looked around, and saw Uncle. He bounded towards her, and the ape and the human girl hugged each other tightly. Tay started to cry. The orang-utan, ragged and thin after his long, lonely trek from the coast, rocked her in his long shaggy arms, stroking her hair. There's a time when you daren't let go, there's a time when tears have to attack you unawares . . . There's a time when you know it is all right to cry. At last Tay wiped her eyes. Totally unafraid, she unpeeled Uncle's powerful arms from round her, and looked him in the face.

'Uncle, I left you alone with strangers. I know it was wrong. I understand now. You'd taken me back to the other humans. Then you'd done what you knew Clint wanted, and you didn't want to go on. You were mourning for him. That's why you were the way you were, wasn't it? That's why you wouldn't take any notice of me—'

Pam came over to them. Uncle didn't move away, but he grunted warily. 'Hnnh?'

'It's all right, Uncle,' said Tay, taking hold of the ape's hand. 'She's our friend. She had to keep you shut up because of Phillipe. She couldn't help that. And she's *not* going to send you away to live in a zoo.' She stared at her gene-mother, defiantly.

'Hmm,' said Pam. 'I don't know about that. We'll decide what's best—'

Uncle made a long-lip, eyeing Tay sideways, as if he understood every word.

'He wants to stay with me,' said Tay. 'I know he does. He came back here because I'd left him alone. But he can't stay in the forest, and he doesn't want to die, so he has to stay with me and you. He needs me, and I owe him. And I expect you to fix it.'

Uncle looked at Pam, with wise round eyes. She could have sworn he was looking at her as one adult to another; and that they both knew it was Tay who needed Uncle. Tay was pleading, like a child, for herself as much as for her beloved companion. Uncle, the only link with her past, was the key to Tay's happiness, and her return to life.

'All right,' Pam said, speaking to both of them. 'I don't know how, but we'll do it. We'll work something out. I promise.'

Uncle grunted again, this time in what sounded like satisfaction. He freed his hand from Tay's grip, touched the green branches that covered Donny's grove, with his long graceful fingers, and brought his fingers to his lips, again and again. Ouch, ouch, ouch.

'We aren't going to leave Donny behind,' Tay told him. 'I wish we could, in a way. But we can't. That's what we're here for, Uncle, as well as finding you—'

The ape seemed to follow this explanation. He squatted down, picked up one of the branches, put it aside, and started tugging at the stones underneath.

'Hey, no!' exclaimed Pam, shocked. 'No, not you! Don't do that! You don't have to do that. The soldiers will do the work, we only had to show them the place. Leave it, Uncle! We have to take Tay away from here—' He paid no attention. Thin and worn as he was, he was still immensely strong. He had no trouble lifting one of the river boulders that he'd put in place, weeks ago. He tossed it aside and looked at the woman and girl, making a crooning sound.

'That's his Clint noise!' cried Tay. 'What is it, Uncle? What are you trying to tell us?'

'*Clint!*' said Uncle again. He pulled out, from behind the stone that he'd removed, a square bundle of black plastic. He sniffed it all over, and hugged it in his arms.

'Oh!' gasped Tay, amazed. 'It's Clint's package!'

'The package you told me was lost crossing the river?' said Pam.

'That's what I thought. That's when I noticed it was gone. I emptied the rucksack, after we'd had to swim for it, to see what we'd lost, and Clint's package wasn't there—'

'He must have decided it belonged here,' said Pam, softly. 'You were burying Donny. Uncle must have decided that this cairn should be Clint's memorial, too . . .' She hunkered down, putting herself on a level with the ape. 'Uncle, may I take that? I don't know how much you understand, cousin. But that's Clint's last work. He didn't want it buried. He wanted it to live.'

'Uncle wants to live, too,' whispered Tay. 'He came back to Donny's grave to die, because he thought I didn't need him any more. But I'm here, and so he wants to live. I think . . . I think Clint told him he had to look after us, no matter what—'

'Your choice, Uncle,' said Pam, holding out her hands. 'Do you want me to have that?'

Uncle grunted, looked at the sky, and handed the package over.

'Thank you.'

She tore through the wrapping with shaking hands. There

172

were computer disks inside, and a stack of typescript. 'Ah,' she breathed. 'It's . . . I think this is Clint's new book.'

'Is that important?'

'He was such a scatterbrain. We only have his notes, and an early draft. This is the whole thing. Yes, it's important. It's something saved, Tay. It's something saved.'

Pam went to tell the soldiers that Donny's grave had been found, leaving Tay and Uncle to make their last farewells alone. 'This will be Donny's grave forever,' said Tay. 'It doesn't matter where they take his body, or if we never come back. Donny will always be here, and we will be with him, by this stream in the forest.'

We will always be with Donny, agreed Uncle. He'll always be with us.

And if Tay made up his words, still it wasn't make-believe.

The spirit of the great forest, distilled into this narrow valley, folded its arms around the river beach, and two mourners, and a cairn buried in green boughs. Tay knew that this time there was nothing left undone, and it really was farewell.

They went to join Pam, hand in hand. The soldiers came and did what had to be done.

The Inheritors

The kidnapped staff from the Refuge were not released. They were traced, after several more weeks, to a rebel stronghold in the highlands. All those who had survived the weeks of captivity survived when the Kandanese army surrounded the place and convinced the rebels to surrender. Before that time, Mary and Ben Walker's bodies had been recovered from the ruins in the Refuge clearing, and Clint's friends learned that Clint had been 'executed' the same day that he was captured. The forest fires of that summer, although they had seemed so terrible on the ground, made only a small scar on the thousands of hectares of remaining forest. The Sultan of Kandah, once more secure in power, set aside another Lifeforce reserve, and in time Tessa Mahakam became warden of a new Refuge. After the publicity around the events of that summer, and his tragic death, Dr Suritobo's book, *The Forest People: Our Gentle Cousins*, sold ten million copies in the first week it was published. All the profits went to wildlife conservation.

Taylor Five Walker travelled half-way round the world, with her gene-mother and the bodies of her dead, to England. There was a funeral, and a memorial service, at which a lot of people said they were very sorry, and what wonderful people Tay's mum and dad had been. Pam returned to her work after that, but Tay stayed in England for a while, living with her aunt and uncle in Southampton, and going to visit the cousins who were her only relatives on her mum's side. She was one of the three 'Lifeforce Teenagers' willing to talk to the media. While she was in England she gave a few interviews, for the newspapers and on radio (she refused to appear on television).

'Lifeforce gave me my childhood,' she said. 'They didn't have to do that. They could have kept us away from everything human and normal, and studied us to death. But they weren't like that. They were real, human people. They did what they did because they thought they had no alternative, and they tried to do it well. I'll always be glad that I lived in the great forest, and knew the red apes in their natural home. I'll always be glad I had those years, with Mum and Dad and Donny, even though it ended so terribly. And I'm very glad to have been partly the means of giving M-389 medicines to the world. Now I'm going to try and go on having a wonderful time . . . I'm going to *live*, do good things, and be happy, because that's what my mum and dad and Donny would have wanted. I'm going to have an amazing life.'

Several months after the events of that summer, she was back in Singapore. She was going to live with her gene-mother until she went to the Inheritors College, where she would meet Takami Three Abe again, and probably the three other extraordinary, ordinary teenagers. She walked into the bustling arrivals hall at Changi airport, and her heart stopped. She remembered another day, a different, small and shabby airport hall. She heard again her brother's clear voice, shouting joyfully, 'Hey! There's my sister!'

No Donny.

But Pam Taylor was there, and with her, looking as

175

plump and well-brushed as a shaggy, shambling orang-utan can ever be, was Uncle. The girl and the ape stood looking into each other's eyes, remembering everything. The gibbons in the bamboo stand. A cake with green and yellow icing. The voices forever stilled, from the chorus that had sung 'By the Rivers of Babylon', coming down from the outcrop on Mary Walker's birthday. Nothing would be lost, because everything would be remembered, and woven into the tapestry that was Uncle, and that was Taylor Five. They told each other this, silently. Then they turned, hand in hand, to face the unknown future.

Author's Note

There is no Kandah State on the island of Borneo. There isn't a 'dry north east corner' on Borneo either; my descriptions of the savannah country are taken from Baluran National Park in North East Java. But it's true that most of the rainforests on Borneo and Sumatra are gone, and it's true that the orang-utans are almost certainly doomed to lose their natural habitat, very soon.

Also by Ann Halam

The Powerhouse

'The face looked at Maddy. I saw its empty eyes gleam . . . Somebody screamed and screamed. I think it was me.'

Robs, Jef and Maddy: three friends who just wanted to make music together. How could one summer change their lives the way it did? Maddy and Robs survived, but only just. And the nightmare that happened in the Powerhouse will live with them forever.

'superbly packaged horror' *Books Magazine*
'worth twenty Point Horrors' *School Librarian*

The Fear Man

A dreadful secret hangs over the house in Roman Road. What is it that keeps drawing Andrei to it? And what is the unknown presence that seems to be stalking the family? Constantly on the run from a father he has never known, Andrei is living a nightmare. A compelling story of vampires, magicians and creatures of darkness.

'brilliantly written . . . a very powerful and affecting book' *BBC Radio 4 Treasure Islands*

The Haunting of Jessica Raven

'Darkness. A cold, foul-smelling darkness. Somewhere a child was screaming.'

Mysterious things start happening to Jessica when, on holiday in France, she meets a group of ragged children. She cannot work out where they come from, but when she meets their leader, an older boy called Jean-Luc, she begins to realise that they may hold the key to her brother's fatal illness.

'. . . a novel of singular completeness and perfection. With it Ann Halam confirms her standing as one of the most exciting of emerging talents' *Junior Bookshelf*

Crying in the Dark

'She didn't know why she had such a strange feeling that they shouldn't have left her alone – but suddenly she understood what the ghosts were trying to tell her. She could make the Madisons wish they'd never been born . . .'

Bullied and abused by her adoptive family Elinor retreats into the restless, vengeful past that haunts their seventeenth-century home. At first it's a way to escape, but soon she's a prisoner and the price of her freedom is something too terrible to contemplate.

'An excellent and compelling ghost story . . .'
The Guardian

The N.I.M.R.O.D. Conspiracy

'*Dear Mum – I'm wedged under the sea-defences, most of me has been eaten by the fishes. Love, Stacey*' . . .

Stacey vanished three years ago. She's dead. It's Alan's fault. He knows. But Mum refuses to believe it – her endless search for her little daughter leads them first to NIMROD, and then into a criminal underworld of deceit and conspiracies, burglary, blackmail and terrible danger. NIMROD wields a mysterious power. But *who* are they really? What do they know about Stacey? What can they possibly want from Alan and his mum?

'a chilling, exciting story' *Our Schools Magazine*

Don't Open Your Eyes

Blood red eyes. Bare bone. Ragged, rotting flesh. No escape.

Something awful has happened to Martin. You'd think it would be all over – after the joyriding, the crash, Martin's tragic death. He was only fifteen.

But Diesel, who was so desperate to make sure that Martin's final resting place was somewhere he feels safe, knows this is just the start of something too terrifying even to think about.

WARNING: DON'T OPEN YOUR EYES unless you are sure you dare read this utterly spinechilling horror story.

Dr Franklin's Island

What's it like to see your best friend transformed into a bird in front of your eyes? What's it like to know it's your turn next?

On a tiny tropical island the palm fringed beaches hide a terrible secret. Beyond the azure waters and white sands is Dr Franklin's 'hospital'.

Miranda, Semi and Arnie, sole survivors of a plane crash, are about to become his next victims. He's been waiting for them. They're perfect specimens for his experiments in genetic engineering.

A horrifying, fascinating story of three friends who leave their human forms to become fish and fowl – nothing like it has ever been written before.